NOTES FROM THE GHOSTWRITER

NOTES FROM

THE GHOSTWRITER

October City Vampire Tales, Volume 1

Written by
Kaytee Thrun

Cover and Interior Artwork by
Alberto Aprea

october city press

Notes From The Ghostwriter, October City Vampire Tales, Volume 1
Copyright © 2007 *Kaytee Thrun*

Published 2007
October City Press
www.octobercitypress.com

Cover and Interior Artwork by Alberto Aprea

ISBN: 978-0-6151-3883-1

Printed in the United States of America

Meet Devin Marks, a struggling romance novel ghostwriter who receives a new assignment from her publisher to ghostwrite a novel based on a vampire TV show. Worried about her lack of experience in that area, her publisher enlists the help of a mysterious and dark stranger who claims to be an occult and vampire expert. When the research begins, the stranger's true face is revealed, along with a dark hidden agenda stemming from World War II. He has her deciding between the lonely world she knew and her newfound bloody legacy as a vampire hunter.

Dedications

JoAnn Thrun (ma), thank you for trusting in all of my eccentricities and creative endeavors.

Cinder. 23 ½ years. I love you. I have no words.

"Uncle Bill" Swick, Ed and Julie Rader, Jeff Zimmerman, Julie Carey, Dena Wolferman, Steve Coates, and Wendy Smith - all of you, thank you for staying. You all remind me who I am. Joe G. Armondo, Larry and Kim Armondo, Papa, Alberto Aprea, Domino, Buffy, Lyli, Zane, Gabriel, and the other Lily, Zerow, & David Thrun. There are all kinds of inspirations.

> "What have you done today to make you feel proud?"
> - *Proud,* Heather Small

Remember to thank those
who inspire you…

Thank You

KT

Chapter One

Night wrapped its cold slender fingers around the thick hot frame of day. The sun slowly disappeared like it always did. As predictable and resilient as the clock that ticked in perfect time on the living room wall.

Devin slid forward on her wooden desk chair a few inches. It was noticeably uncomfortable, but that kept her focused. She settled back into a less painful position. Her fingers clacked hard against the keys on her laptop. She was getting back into a writing rhythm, she thought. The words were starting to flow out of her fingertips. Thank God. She can do this. She can finish this stupid book.

I shalt make it to the cabin in time, Lily thought as she raced down the beach towards the bluff. Her long flowing white dress blowing in the cool sea air. The faint image of her curves making their way through the thinness of the fabric.

"Oh, Lucias my love," she cried as she saw him in the distance.

A flicker of rapid orange dawn glowed about his brazen shoulders. His muscles rippling underneath his skin. His hair blew behind him in slow motion breeze.

She outstretched her arms and met his warm embrace.

"My dear one," he exclaimed, "the prophet foretold to me that I would never again view your splendor."

His voice was deep and swollen in his throat. He touched her cheek with his strong rough hands.

She shuddered at his touch. It both cooled and warmed her skin. Small breaths escaped her lungs and came out in whimpers of ecstasy.

"Everyone needs just three things in their life, my dear love. Something to feed their heart, something to feed their soul, and something to feed their pocketbook. That is why I returned." she said.

He reached into the pocket of his open vest and pulled out a small heart-shaped pendant. He pressed it against the crease between her breasts.

She melted into him. She winced in ecstasy.

No, not ecstasy. She used that word too many times. Devin stopped typing and rested her head on the back of her chair, lifting her fingers off the keyboard. A loose curl escaped the scrunchy that held up her shoulder length brown hair and fell in her eyes. She tucked it back behind her ear. Need a haircut.

She winced in agony.

No.

She winced in...lust?

No!

Ex-treme...somethings.

Ugh! She couldn't think of the right word. Total writers block tonight.

She slammed down the lid on her laptop hard, pushed it forward on the desk, and leaned back in her chair. The wooden legs creaked as she tilted back on just the two rear legs and put her hands over her tired eyes, exhaling deeply.

This latest romance novel was killing her. It was taking much longer to write than the normal few weeks it usually takes. After so many, another can be a killer. She felt as if all the creativity had been sucked out of her by an all-consuming mystical space-vacuum.

God! She couldn't even think creatively. How awful.

She needed something to get her back into writing mode. Something to energize her, only she had no idea what that was. These romance novel characters are so boring and clichéd. Each and every one is exactly the same as the one before. The only differences were where they lived, a castle, on the beach, the mountains, or what they did for a living, a knight, a cowboy, a sailor. All the same torrid romance stories with perfect long haired men airbrushed on the soft covers. It was so shallow.

She lifted her numb fingers like claws in front of her face. Curling them tightly into fists. She had been typing for so many hours that she lost track of the time. The sun had peeked its way under the horizon and the lights of the nighttime city had sprung up outside her windows. Darkness again greets her.

She moved to greet it as well.

She stood up, letting the wooden chair legs rattle on the hard floor. She walked slowly towards the windows. They stretched the entire length of the room from floor to ceiling. Small colorful lights echoed across the tops of skyscrapers and even smaller ones rolled down the streets below like lightning bugs scurrying down some secret path in the darkness.

She felt so alone. This apartment sometimes surrounded her like a cage. She was forced day after day to sit within it and write these mindless sagas while the watching eyes outside took notes and judged. She peered out into the darkness wondering who might be looking back at her.

The city had a reputation and she let her anxieties get the best of her sometimes. It made her always alone.

"Devin Alison Marks, who are you?" She whispered under her breath.

She kept repeating that question over and over in her head.

This is not like you to sit here and take this kind-of treatment. After all, you are 26 years old. You are not a baby anymore; you can make your own decisions. Stand up, be tough and tall.

She stood up as straight and as tall and she could and held it for a few seconds. Then, she returned to her always slouching stance.

She turned and walked back towards her desk. She flopped back down onto the hard chair. It shocked her spine.

"Ugh, need that chiropractor."

And she could afford it now. Now that she moved to the city. It had called to her. After getting her degree in Journalism at a small local state college, she found herself thirty miles north of nowhere and interviewing for jobs. She wanted to live a TV-like big city life.

"Never should've watched *Sex in the City*."

She got a job at a second rate local neighborhood newspaper and began covering the boring facts of middle America. Exciting stories like the minutes of town hall meetings, water treatment, and road construction clouded her head. It seemed so long ago.

The potholes on Armondo Drive will be filled by the end of the business month. The streetlight at Lake and Hillside will be replaced. Boring. Always so boring.

Less than a year after starting that job, she became a fulltime novelist. A dream job that just landed in her lap. It appeared out of nowhere and she had always wondered if that was some weird fate or some magick.

After all, she was sitting in the middle of a pretty sweet apartment. She looked quickly around the room and nodded a slight approval. Not many girls her age had it so good, so why didn't it feel good? Maybe because she was the only one that ever even saw the inside of this place.

She exhaled and looked down at the floor between her knees. Hardwood floors and real ones too, not that laminated plastic junk made to look like real wood. She drew her eyes up slowly following the crease in the corner of the wall to the top. Vaulted ceilings with exposed pipe and rafters, a real urban loft feel. Soft velvety tan walls.

Along a lone wall hung that painting she bought last year at an art gallery. It was by an artist named Macan. The figure of a cat ensnared by leaves and roses. Very colorful, but still very dark. She imagined the artist was this mysterious man with long jet black hair and deep unimaginable eyes. He ventured out only at night, wearing all black. She loved that painting. It was worth the money. It helped inspire her, but for some reason not tonight.

She turned her head to the right. Brick walls and the front door, a big and heavy metal sliding door. She panned slowly to the left, a wall of windows watching the city. Floor to ceiling. The room had a light contemporary design opaqued by the darkness of the artwork.

In addition to the Macan, there were several figural sculptures in metal. Long, lean, and nude. It was a way for

Devin to show her sexuality and feminine side without being crude. Art is a way for you to do that. To be anyone if only for a few moments and for the sake of art. A large mirror with a border made of pottery stood alone on a vacant wall. Very open and airy. Very lofty.

Most days I like it here.

It even echoed when she got so frustrated writing that she screamed at the top of her lungs. After days of her mind racing with silly romantic thoughts and the realization that she had not spoken in those days. It exploded to the surface in shrieks. She would collapse on her couch in tears, letting it all out.

It only bothered the neighbors to her right, a middle-aged couple that thought moving to a funky artsy community would make them more edgy. They remained tightly wound and damaged, just like when they arrived. It didn't work. She rarely conversed with any of her neighbors. She kept such weird hours as a writer that she never saw anyone.

Devin felt wound too tightly tonight too. She needed something to release this pent up stress. Her boss was driving her slowly towards the peak of insanity and she had no outlets of release.

What an ass my boss is.

But this job did pay her well and for right now, there was not a thing she could do about it. Not for two more years at least. Not until Baxter cut her loose from her contract. That seemed like it would never happen.

It was a weird feeling of being owned, being a possession of someone else. With the romantic novel twist, it felt very like she was a woman many years ago forced into a subservient position to the men in her life. Viewed as something to toile away and something to screw. Something right out of one of the novels she wrote. The female lead was always in the submissive position. There was something so romantic about a time when your knight or cowboy or master would come and take you away and ravish you. She wasn't sure if she always felt this way or if writing romance novels made her see things differently. Maybe she would never know.

Maybe it was fate.

Maybe magick.

The everyday boring newspaper job ended one day with a great deal of fate. She was out covering a zoning meeting when she first saw him. He sat in the back of the room and his eyes never left her throughout the entire meeting. It made her feel dirty. When the meeting ended and the citizens filed out of the village building like disappointed cattle, he came up to her. He smelled of cheap hard liquor and cigars. His suit looked years old and too tight for his middle-aged beer bellied body. His hair had gone more to salt and pepper and his round cheeks were tinted red.

"I'm familiar with your work," he told her.

"Really." She said, wondering how exciting it must have been to read all about potholes and garbage pick-up.

"I own a small local publishing company. My name is Jake Baxter."

He offered her a job on the spot. That was something that had never happened to her before.

With reluctance, she accepted after she read the offer letter. Real money now. She found herself strangely out of journalism and into Baxter Publishing. A risky, but exciting maneuver. It felt big city and romantic, just like she dreamed about.

Just like the work she would write. Baxter employed several dozen staff writers and had a string of so-so popular writers with grocery checkout line recognizable names. The good old-fashioned trade paperback book housewife loving romance predict-a-byte theme. They flooded out of the publishing house one after another, month after month. The all sounded exactly the same with the same desire for love buried in the heart of every reader.

It was nothing like what Devin wanted, but after Jake Baxter, a.k.a. President and Chief Editor of the house, offered her a full-time job as a staff ghostwriter, she couldn't say no. Their current ghostwriter disappeared a few weeks before and they were desperate for a replacement. Almost all of their big name writers wrote only half of their best sellers.

The money rolled in like water and the jobs were easy. Ghostwrite romance novels for successful authors. Easy. At first. Now, the money went quickly and so did her love for the work.

Romance was something she used to not understand. Maybe she still didn't understand it now. Maybe having to emulate all this romance day after day has made her mis-interpret what it really is about. Real romance never played a part in her life.

Coming from a middleclass family, the job smelled of the stability and safety Devin longed for. She never went without, but could see now that her parents feared not being able to retire at 65. Her father was without work half the time as a cabinetmaker and her mother was a stay at home mom for her and her adopted brother. They were not a close family and the financial problems always seemed to hang overhead like a shroud. With money always tight, nothing was ever safe and stable. She longed for that feeling. She longed to get it on her own. Love never played a part in that. Romance never played a part in that either.

So, this seemed like a fated situation. Before she could blink, she was moved into a great loft apartment, on Baxter's recommendation and typed away the great American romance novel day after day.

Piece of cake right? Until a year into the gig when she really read the fine print of her contract. She was not allowed to publish anywhere, but through Baxter Publishing for the duration of the six-year contract. Locked in tight. No loopholes.

She first discovered this when bringing a first draft novel into Baxter's office one morning. He turned it down flat without even glancing through a page or two for show. Arrogance abound. And she knew it was a good novel too. It was about a woman scientist that worked on a team trying to increase the growth patterns of vegetation to help solve the world's hunger problems. Unfortunately, a lab accident let out the experiment and the world sunk into a dark jungle age. Dangerous cats roamed the streets hunting for victims. It was kind-of a horror story. A stretch for Devin, but she loved it with all her heart. Something so different than these bubbly romance stories. Now it sat in a drawer collecting dust. *White Fur, Gold Eyes, Dead Cats, and Water.* Some day it will be published. She was certain of that.

"Won't you even read it?" Devin pleaded with Baxter.

"You will write for our big name writers and put out the stories we want you to and that's that," he stammered. "If and when we want your name on anything, we'll tell you."

He dropped her manuscript onto the desk hard.

"Right now your name is nothing and makes us nothing. Squat. Now get your ass back to work."

And that was it. She remembered his words completely. They were burned into her memory entirely. Possession.

So was the fact that she was to ghostwrite forty novels over the course of six years, all to be published under the names of other writers. Writers like Catherine McGovern-Salem, one of Baxter's most profitable novelists, who incidentally only wrote half of her bestsellers. Devin had penned two herself for Catherine, but reaped none of the true benefits. The book signings, the TV interviews, the royalty checks that rolled in one after another. She longed for that recognition.

Her only chance to get published under her own name in the next two years was for Baxter to have a gross change of heart.

It was highly unlikely. He had no heart.

Empty. From the top of his salt and pepper hair to the bottom of his worn out old shoes.

Ringgggg! The phone rings sharply, plucking her out of her half daydream state. She shakes it off like a cold sweat. Reality.

She sits up straight in the chair shockingly and brushes the loose curls out of her eyes again. The chair legs rock back and forth against the cold floor. The sound echoes loudly through the room. She looks around the desk for the ringing cell phone. She finds it under a stack of scribbled handwritten book notes. She fumbles to hit the call button and stop the Latin dance ring tone her brother programmed.

"Hello?" she stutters out.

"Devy, baby, who's your favorite Jacky-boy?" a grumbly voice chattered on the other end of the line.

"Hey," she responded disappointed that he bought her out of her daydream state. "What's up?"

The voice on the other end was Jake Baxter himself, but of course it was. It always was. He always took that special interest in her and wanted to handle things personally. She hated that.

"I have a new job for you baby and you're gonna love it"

"Lucky me."

"Come on down to the office tonight. I'll have all the dzzz and tails for ya then."

"What time?"

"About 7ish babe."

"I'll be there."

She clicked the end button on her cell phone and tossed it back atop the pile of papers. She left him no room to continue the conversation. If she did, it would undoubtedly turn to sex. She lets out an exhausted exhale. Too bad they have no Human Resources department.

She would be there on time, as always. Just like she was always at home. Right where she was trapped. Maybe this new writing job wouldn't be as bad as some of the others. Maybe the pitch will be good, something new. Maybe not a romance novel for once, maybe a crime drama with a subtle romantic twist. Maybe anything, but of course it wouldn't be.

She opened the top right drawer of her desk and took out a small blue lined spiral notebook. She flipped it open to the center and wrote the number 27 on the top of the blank page.

Alien Love Manbots crash land on Earth in the 1800's and stumble across a secret mission full of women studying to become nuns.

"Ppfft, excellent."

Each time Baxter called her in for a pitch meeting, she would jot down her most outrageous plotline guess. Sometimes, she was not too far off. We'll see this time.

She closed the notebook and tossed it back into the drawer. She slammed it closed hard. One of these times, she will be dead on.

She let out a deep breath, placed her hands on the arms of the chair, and pushed herself up and out and walked towards her bedroom. Her socks shuffled against the flooring. She thought she had better change into something a little more presentable before heading downtown.

She stopped as she entered her bedroom and stood in front of the full-length mirror. She leaned to the right and dropped her best super model pose complete with pouting lips and hands on hips. The yellow light from the living room lamp haloed her in the mirror frame. She tried as hard as she could to see herself better than this life, but the truth always seemed to seep through.

My God, had she really been wearing these pants for three days? Her mushy plaid jammy pants had officially become her everything everyday pants and her not-matching dark green band t-shirt with accenting red canned spaghetti stain really made the ensemble. Her brown hair was knotted-up in a scrunchy on the top of her head. Dirty. Her green eyes looked swollen and tired.

Did I shower yesterday?

She sniffed the air, as if she could tell the difference anymore. *This*, she thought as she gestured towards the mirror, *was the biggest drawback of being a work at home writer.* She never left her loft anymore. But what did it matter anyway? Just an average looking midwestern girl doesn't stand out anywhere. No one noticed.

She had better take a quick shower before she got dressed. She tossed off her stylish outfit and let the clothes land on top of the huge pile of dirty ones slowly staking their claim on the bedroom floor.

She hopped in the shower for a fast five minutes, barely rinsing the soap off her skin and slipped into her favorite jeans and a plain red t-shirt. She brushed through her hair once with a wide tooth comb and replaced the tired old scrunchy that she wore before. No make-up needed, she thought. She stopped for a quick second at the full-length mirror again. She barely remembered what it was like to care about her appearance. It had been so long since anybody *saw* her in a way that would make her care.

Slipping on her shoes and grabbing her jacket and keys, she headed out the front door.

She only had about 15 minutes to make it downtown and the train took 10 minutes. If she caught the next one, she would just make it in time.

The air outside was crisp, but not really cold. She cut across the dark street, between two passing cars and jogged the half a block to the transit stop. The neighborhood seemed eerily deserted for this time of night. She heard the train whistle in the distance and knew she was right on time. She ran up the old metal stairs. They banged in the quiet air.

The train approached by way of one bright yellow light that looked like a bug zapper. It was almost as bright as the disappearing sun that was hiding its way just beneath the horizon.

The large metal machine grumbled to a slow stop. It hissed and steamed as it pulled up in front of her. She and three other waiting passengers stepped on when the doors slid open like on Star Trek.

That image always made riding public transportation seem cooler to Devin. Like some futuristic world where she was smarter and more important. That or the desire to write something other than romance was starting to cloud her judgment. She was not a big science fiction fan, but anything seemed better that the fakeness of all this love.

Darkness. Mystery. Passion. Death. Something to breathe the life back into her. Something to make her feel again. Feel anything at all.

Pant. Hisssss.

The doors hissed closed in front of her and the quick 10-minute rolled down the tracks towards downtown and her next assignment.

Chapter Two

She swung at the heavy door handle and stepped into the cold grey office building. Her footsteps echoed off the floor, as does the slamming door behind her. The offices are near emptied after 5 p.m., so no one is ever around. Baxter always asked her to come in late. She knew the emptiness of the lobby like the back of her hand. The faux marble walls are slightly shiny and smudged with fingerprints. A thousand daytime visitors that travel unnoticed. In the center, a small reception desk, never occupied. No one and nothing else.

She strolled to the elevator, *2 minutes early*, looking down at her watch. She smiled to herself satisfied and pushed the up button. She waited anxiously. She wanted to get this over with quickly.

The elevator door dings and slipped open quietly. As she stepped inside, she felt a cold rush of air brush behind her. Devin turned sharply, but saw no one in the lobby.

Strange.

She settled in the middle of the elevator and pressed the button for the 4th floor. The door pants closed.

Elevator music crackles through a poorly designed speaker system. She hums softly to herself as the ride creeps upward. Why do they always make elevator versions of great songs? They never hold up like the originals.

The door opened and she made her way down the long hallway. The fluorescent lighting flickers on and off overhead. The carpeting was thick and old, a mix of dark blood red and pumpkin orange. *Probably a big color in the 60's* she thought. That old building smell was everywhere. It rubbed off on her.

Poor ventilation. The walls were a dirty beige, as if they had been stained with nicotine over the years. She ran her finger down the wall towards her destination. It picked up stray dust.

She pushed open the large wooden door to Baxter Publishing. It creaked slowly and loudly as she entered.

The faint sound of conversation lilted from down the hallway where *his* office is located.

She cautiously took small steps towards the sound. She did not want to interrupt an important meeting, but also wanted a heads up if the conversation was about her. The journalist in her heart could never pass up the opportunity to get some advance information. At least something more interesting then village hall notes or new parking permits. She was always listening.

Just as she focused in on the sounds, the voices stopped and she too stopped dead in her tracks. She held her breath waiting for a sound.

Baxter's office door was pushed open by a large heavy hand. She waited to see who was attached to it.

"Devy baby!"

She let out a light sigh as she saw Baxter standing in front of her with his arms outstretched.

"Come inside sweetie," he gestured.

She went inside and dropped herself casually on the old brown leather couch. It made that uncomfortable squeaking sound. She settled into a sink in the middle and waited for his new pitch. She hoped inside that it would be something more interesting than her last few assignments.

Baxter took his usual spot leaning on the edge of his desk with his arms folded like an angry schoolteacher. He gave her a daunting look, like the bad student. In his sick mind he probably played out some tired old schoolgirl fantasy with her.

Pervert.

Too damn bad the paychecks were so good.

"I have a new job for you," he taunted. His smile twisted up as he begged for her anticipation.

"Who were you just talking to?" she asked him, as she noticed that they were alone in the room.

"No one," he said with a stumbling chortle, quickly distorting out of the crooked smile. "Just no one, babe."

She gazed around for a backdoor that she never remembered seeing. There wasn't one. Puzzling. Was Baxter in here talking to himself? It wouldn't surprise Devin in the slightest if he had gone completely mad. He was half way there when they met.

"Anyway, you are gonna love this new job. It is what you have been waiting for, a non-romance gig."

She gave him that satisfied look that he had hoped for. Inside her nerves jumbled with excitement. A non-romance book, that could mean anything, but no matter what, it was better than the love lost words she tried to pull from her bored mind everyday.

"Really?" she sat upright on the couch. The same couch squeak came from beneath her jeans. "Tell me about it."

He paused for a second, soaking up the interest she had. He had a way of making everything seem dirty.

"Well, you know Dena Zimmerman?"

"Yes, well I have seen her books. Kind-of teen mystery stuff, right?"

Dena was one of Baxter Publishing's top non-romance best sellers. She had four novels out so far, each as clichéd as the one before. Each one full of zombies and demons extracted right out of the most common folklore, no originality. Formulaic and full of simple words and simpler ideas. Very young adult writing by a bad author. They sold like crazy.

Yeh, Devin knew her.

"Well, Dena has been caring for her sick husband all year and needs to get out another book ASAP," Baxter said. "She has a basic idea for a storyline, but now she's taken ill too. If we miss a season, we lose her fan base babe."

Lose money is what he meant. Devin shifted uncomfortably on the couch. She hoped she never became as money focused as Baxter had become.

"This one will be a killer too. A writer friend of hers was asked to write a story based on the TV show *Buffy the Vampire Slayer*. She enlisted Dena to co-write with her. Can you dig that crazy shit babe?" he asked.

She lifts her eyebrows in silent response.

"Then, the friend gets really sick and cannot lift a finger to write and Dena gets the deal to write the whole thing. Their time constraints forced it. Lucky ducky break for us. Bad break for the friend."

He sounded too excited. Shouldn't he be more worried about the health of one of his writers? And what about her friend?

"Like a crazy epidemic babe," Baxter said. "Dena is totally housebound and can barely move. Hope she gets better, but in the mean, we gotta rock this number. It is a sure thing. That *Buffy* deal, that was one of the biggest sci-fi moneymakers ever on the tube. We get 50% of the royalties for Dena. A guaranteed seller. There's just one thing. We have very little time."

Time was never an issue with Devin. The romance stories flooded out of her like a river. But this? This was different.

Wasn't that what I wanted?

"Can you pen this one sugar?"

When she first heard it was Dena Zimmerman, she figured she could knock out a so-so story about ghosts in a haunted mansion or maybe zombies, but a vampire story based on a TV show? How was she going to do that? Writing from television, she has to be fact smart. The details are critical. One wrong step and you lose the reader.

"I don't know Bax, I never watched the show and don't know a thing about it," she answered. "I don't think I can pull off the accuracy on this one. I can get character names, but what about all the facts. That show was on for like years and years."

She knew that there were hundreds of books out with the characters and about all the specifics of the show. The fans study these facts and even role play. This was something she couldn't just fake her way through. She had gotten good at faking romance, but not like this. Not this time.

"Well, I thought about that and I have a solution. I have an offer that might make you jump at this job."

"What Bax?"

"If you write this book and do a knock-out job worthy of our Miss Zimmerman, I'll let you publish one of those stories you wrote under your own name."

Devin sat letting his words soak in for a minute. Did she hear him right? One of her own books? No way.

"You will publish one of my novels? Mine, as in not ghostwritten, as in mine *my* books?" she asked.

"Yes," he responded matter of factly. "But I need a first class job on this Dena deal. And in regards to your lack of vampire knowledge, I have a solution for that too. Don't I always take care of you babe? I got you a little research help."

Baxter snapped his fingers twice like he was calling his dog. It echoed in the old fashioned carved wood corners of the room. Baxter waited for something. An impatient, yet nervous look glazed over his fat red cheeks.

Devin felt that same cold rush of air that she felt when entering the elevator. She turned to the left towards the office door to see a shadowy figure brush by her and settle in the tall wingback chair in the far corner of the room. It seemed as if he was just the wind.

"This is Julian," Baxter said gesturing towards the figure, coughing the words out as if they were filled with dust. "He is my all-things horror science fiction gothic research expert."

That was his fancy way of saying occult expert. He struggled for the right words that both explained and failed to insult this mysterious stranger.

"Devin. It's a pleasure to meet you."

She nodded hello, unable to actually get any words out. Her eyes instead trailed up the wall nervously.

Think about anything but him.

She kept her eyes up. Overhead were hundreds of books lining a wall of wooden shelves. Every book Baxter had published and a hundred more he wished he had. An old-fashioned floor lamp stood in the corner and shadowed everything in the room in an eerie glow. Baxter liked his mood lighting. Above his desk hung a portrait of a woman naked. The iridescent color of her skin glowed in the dim lighting. It was sexy, but in a dirty way. Just like Baxter. It made her blush. She worried the stranger noticed.

Just relax.

Devin breathed in deeply and looked at the man straight on. He was tall and lean with a runner's frame. He had wispy dark blond hair that fell around his face like he was stuck in a perfect breeze. His eyes were sticking blue green and his features long and cut. He wore all black and had that 90's Gothic look about him, with something buried in that smile that freaked out and intrigued her at the same time.

"Hello" he said to her with a light chuckle.

It was clear she was uncomfortable talking to men. Her cheeks felt fire red. Just like Baxter's. She was certain they both could see.

God I wish he couldn't see.

His voice was much softer than she thought it would be. By the way he looked, she expected a harsh tone brought from a guttural throat raw from pot smoking and angst. She had no idea whether she responded or not. She was fixated on his eyes.

Baxter began speaking, although she could not hear what he was saying. It was like this stranger was speaking to her through his eyes or his mind. She kept focused on him, even though she tried not to. He drew her in.

I wonder if I look excited?

"Julian is going to give you the 101 on *Buffy* and vampires and everything you need to know to make this book accurate. You will be working side by side," Baxter said.

"With him?" she said slipping back into reality and looking at Baxter.

She was not used to working with anyone on her books. Dirty t-shirts and bad hair days aside, Devin liked her late nights typing alone in her living room. It is how she works best. It unfortunately had become how she lives best too. Alone at night in her loft. Nothing but the familiar echoes.

"You know, I really don't need a collaborator, maybe just some notes and facts," she said. "Just the details that I need to make it right and character bios and stuff. I can handle the rest myself."

"I can handle the rest…blah blah. Are you even listening to me? Do you want to publish your own damn book or what?" Baxter asked, this time with a twinge of anger in his voice.

Back to reality.

"Of course I do, but…"

"Then listen, Julian will teach you everything there is to know about vampires and all that crap and you will listen and learn and pen the best Dena Zimmerman by end of next month. That is my decision. Are we done here?"

He stared at her with that same disconcerting teacher disappointment. Why did he have to talk to her that way with someone else in the room? And a stranger no less. He made her look so stupid.

Julian stood up out of the chair in the corner. He walked towards her. His hair billowed in that non-existent breeze. Then, there was that cold chill again. It tickled her spine softly, almost passionately.

She didn't want to work with anyone, but least of all him. First, he was a man, which made her nervous. She had not dated in years and when she did, she was never really any good at it. Second, he was weird and what could he possibly want to show her? Something she might fear.

Something new.

Something she needed.

"Devin," he said calmly.

Her name rolled off his lips like sex.

"Trust me. I just want to show you what you need to see in order to give the story justice. I have faith in you."

She wanted to have faith in herself. Looking at him, somehow, he made her feel it. His eyes were so blue green after all. They seemed to swim beneath his lids like puddles. She could almost see the water moving as he spoke. Puzzling she thought. And she believed that he did have faith in her. Faith that she did not have in herself lately.

"Well," she hesitated. "I suppose I could do a little research with you. Maybe go over the main points I'll need to focus on."

She smiled a very fake smile and stood up. The leather couch squeaked again in the silence of the room. Her cheeks blushed a little redder.

Baxter reached out with his puffy hand and gave her a festive slap on the back.

She struggled to regain her footing.

At least it was the back this time.

"Very well," he said. "I will leave her in your capable and knowledgeable hands." He gestures Devin forward towards Julian like a present.

Julian curls a hand in towards his chest, as if he is accepting the present. Like he is taking possession of her.

"I thought perhaps we could begin on Thursday."

"Sure, Thursday works. Whenever works. Now…maybe like then…whatever."

How desperate did I just sound?

"You can meet me here."

Julian reached into his coat pocket and pulled out a small piece of parchment with an address scribbled in pencil. His fingers touched hers as they made the exchange. His skin was cold and dry.

"Perhaps around 6 p.m.?"

"Sure," she responded stuffing the parchment into the front left pocket of her jacket. She fidgeted nervously.

Parchment and pencil, so classy. She felt herself blushing again. It had been a while since she had talked to a man that was not a relative, Baxter, or the guy at Starbucks. She could smell man on him, sex and heat. This felt like the first page of one of her cheesy romance novels. She could almost hear the faint sound of horses on the beach in the distance.

"Settled then," said Baxter as he turns and walks around to the back of his desk.

He drops himself into his desk chair and lets out a hefty grunt. He picks up a stack of papers and begins riffling through them with no direction. This was his hint for them to leave.

The sound of their breathing was the only noise in the room for what seemed like minutes. Time moved in slow motion, not allowing them to move or better yet, leave.

"Alright?" Baxter said with a slight snap to his tone.

Devin snapped back to reality. Office, sexy stranger, boss, vampire book, got it. Check. She turned and walked out the office door leaving the stranger there.

He heeded the cue and followed behind her in silence.

She felt uncomfortable knowing he was watching her walk down the hall. It had been so long since she felt watched. Or felt like a woman.

She reached the elevator and hit the down button. The elevator bell dinged and the doors hissed opened. She stepped inside nervously and turned around, expecting to see Julian stepping inside behind her, but he wasn't there.

She held back the doors and peaked out into the hallway. Looking both ways, she did not see him anywhere. He must have taken the stairs, she thought. Four flights is a long walk down. She let go with both hands and the door slid closed. It was cold in the elevator still. That strange breeze remained.

Chapter Three

The cab ride cost $8.54 and Devin felt a hesitation as they pulled up in front of the hotel. She looked back down at the piece of parchment that Julian had given her. She needed to make sure she read the address right.

"Is this 414?" she asked the cab driver.

"Yes, 414 ma'am. Right place."

She handed the driver a ten-dollar bill and got out of the cab and looked up, staring at the 15-story business class hotel in front of her. The windows reflected off the last bit of sun peaking its way under the horizon. It glared yellow orange in Devin's eyes. She squinted and held up her hand in front of her face to block the glare.

Why was he having me meet him at a hotel? She thought. Maybe she misinterpreted something. *Oh, stop it.* She was always looking for the angle. That journalist in her never slept. She took a couple steps towards the hotel.

"Afternoon, any bags miss?" a voice asked.

She looked down and saw a red-faced bellhop smiling gleefully in front of her. His black uniform was stained and worn.

"Any what?"

"Are you here for the convention?"

She gave him a confused look.

He gestured towards a billboard propped up on the sidewalk and leaning against the building front. The black hand painted letters spelled out the words Science Fiction Convention.

"Ugh…you have got to be kidding me."

"Miss?"

"Ugh, no, wait yes. I think," she said. "I'm fine. Thank you."

She smiled and walked through the revolving door and entered the bustling lobby.

Standard business class hotel all right. Cheap sheik patterned carpeting in that weird dirty mauve and a smidge of hardwood flooring. The fake laminate kind, not like what she had in her apartment. Dark wood reservation desk to the right and ugly bellhop uniforms, dusty silk flowers in a large copper bowl on a round marble top table and the faint sound of a piano in the bar down the hallway.

There were probably fifty people buzzing around the lobby like flies. They were all dressed like it was Halloween. The sheer number of people made Devin a little uncomfortable.

Some had on shiny silver spacesuits circa 1950. They were probably made out of rolls and rolls of tin foil. How ridiculous.

Some had pointy ears like that guy from Star Trek and flashed hand gestures like they were in some sort-of galactic gang.

Some wore all black and sported plastic vampire fangs and carried a copy of Anne Rice's *Interview with the Vampire* in their long black manicured fingers. Their solemn Goth looks dripped off them.

Some hung in the corners and looked stoic and medieval. Dark dangerous frightening. No specific science fiction style draped over them, but they owned whatever their style was completely. They made her a little bit nervous.

She felt so out of place. Jeans and a white cotton shirt made her stand out like the librarian in front of a bunch of school kids. She nervously pulled her hair up into a ponytail and sat her sunglasses atop her head. *Maybe I should have worn make-up*, she thought. She grabbed the lapels of her black ¾ length trench coat and pulled the fabric tight to her chest.

"I was starting to wonder about you," a familiar voice said.

A chill trailed up her spine as she turned to the left to see Julian leaning against a wooden column. He smiled and took a step towards her with a jaunty gait. He had a playfulness about him, masked under a dark cold exterior. He was sexy in a way she had never seen before. Looking at him, she had a strange feeling that she would know him for a long time.

"You brought me to a Science Fiction Convention?" she said in an accusatory tone. She tried to regain the facade of self-confidence that she tried so hard to portray.

"A Sci-Fi Con luv," he said in a faux British accent. "Trust me, this will give you the eye-opener you need. Come on, we have much to do."

"Whatever."

He held his left hand out and gestured toward the main hallway.

She paused and then took a long step forward. She felt in a weird way that she would follow him anywhere. It is a shame that they were in such a silly place.

They walked through a maze of convention goers past a myriad of ballrooms filled with vendor tables selling trading cards, magazines, costumes, autographs, and a variety of kitschy statuary and action figures modeled after popular TV shows and movies.

She felt like she had entered the chess club's wet dream in high school. *Xena, Stargate, Buffy, Battlestar Galactica, Lord of the Rings, Star Trek, Vampire the Masquerade.* This was so far of her realm of normalcy. After all, she ran track in high school and college, went to all the dances, dated a baseball player, and like many, shied away from the more weird crowds.

She always wondered what they were really like, outside of that shelter of school.

The high water pants and the thick glasses. The nerds. The black clothes, Hello Kitty purses, and dyed Manic Panic blue hair. The freaks. At least they were something. She was just average. Average looking. Average height and weight. Average wavy shoulder length brown hair. Average green eyes. Average everything. It was exciting to think about playing for a while. Being something. For the same reason she came to the city, but this is a bit too geeky. Even for her. Or maybe, it was a bit too scary for an average midwestern girl.

Time to get real Devin.

Well, in truth, she was on track, but the last one in every race. The other girls never included her in their out of athletic activities. She did go to all the dances, but just with friends. And the baseball player, well he was a great player, but not the most handsome by far. Just average. She always dreamed of just one summer disappearing and showing up at a different school in the fall. Her old friends would never know what happened to her and those who were not her friends, wouldn't even notice. The people at the new school would accept whoever she was when he walked in that first day. Fresh start. Artistic. Everything she had ever wanted to be. Different, loud, creative, independent, strong, brave, and dark. Always with a message. How estranged she felt now in this place, like she was back in school being excluded.

She stopped in the hallway and turned to face Julian. "Yeh, this was fun, but can we go now?"

She coughed to cover the uncomfortable aura that spread around her. Her nerves ticked inside her. She worried that Julian could literally see her blood pulsing in her veins, her rising anxiety attack, her lack of social experience in the late. She tried hard to keep the stoic face she pretended.

"Why do you want to leave so soon?" he asked her. "Before I've had the chance to show you anything."

Geeks like vampires and space aliens? Is that what he wanted to show her? She already knew that. Maybe letting him know would end this silly day.

"My target audience is filled with 30-year old men still living in their mom's basements and collecting comic books?" she said sarcastically. "And the fat girls that never got a date in high school can put on a Renaissance-looking dress and be queen of the ball for one night? I get it. Let's go."

He believed that she thought that.

She believed that.

She felt as if she did not get out the hotel that second, she would burst. Just enough social scene to make her feel alive, but not enough to make her panic.

Julian could see it.

She just knew.

He pushed open the door he was leaning upon. Down a short hallway another door opened as if by itself. A pulse of dark dance music hissed out like steam *hhhhhiiiiisssssssss* and she reluctantly followed him inside.

She'll give him 10 minutes. Tops.

The mood of the room was mysterious and it looked like a nightclub. She could barely remember the feeling of going to clubs years ago with her friends. This place had the same ominous and mysterious feel. There was a dimly lit stage with a DJ spinning industrial dance music and two go-go dancers doing a poor job of gyrating beside him. They were adorned in black leather and mesh. Knee-hi boots swayed.

"This is the Vampire 24 hour Ball," he said. "This is one of the things I wanted to show you."

Julian waved his arm slowly across the length of the room. It seemed as if it took minutes to point to every face, every hider, and every person in the room. It seemed as if they all had time to look back. Like Alice looking through the mirror. Both sides seem to not know about the other, except through a lucid dream.

Many of the people in the room were dressed very Gothic. Long velvet dresses and capes, black hair, ornate jewelry, white faces, and extreme make-up. They stepped right out of fiction, like Bram Stoker's *Dracula*. Why did everyone think that Keanu Reeves was stupid? She adored him. Anyway...

Many others in the room took a more demonish approach. Grotesque facial make-up, fake blood, body parts. Very creature of the night, emphasizing the word creature. Early black and white monster films where the villain was always too evil and bad to love. When the camera lens shook and everything was real. Those actors inspired these costumes.

And yet there were just a few that hung back along the walls and in the corners. They had a solumness like Julian did. Real Goths, Devin thought. Sexy romantic dark wonderful. Two figures groped each other in the corner. Their hands roamed freely and their heads cocked back in pleasure. They both were women. Devin could not stop looking at them, until they turned to look at her.

"You see the different faces people paint on vampires?" Julian asked. "Some see them as horrible evil monsters and some see them as beautiful spirits of the night. You need to write to both audiences, but also look to the further truths."

"Some love the Anne Rice sexy romantic vampires and some love the creepy monster stealing babies image," she chuckled slightly and panned the room. "Got it."

She had seen her fair share of vampire films and had always lumped all images into a similar category. But there was truth to what Julian said. *Interview with the Vampire* was sexy with Lestat and romantic. Old vampire black and whites with long creepy claws and horrific features were very scary and unapproachable.

"What about those people?" she asked as she glanced and cocked her towards the corner dwellers, passing her eyes past the two women once more.

"Those are the celebrities. They are the truth."

She felt a cold breeze blow against her back and she turned quickly to see if a door had been opened. No door. Just the small frail figure of a woman stood behind her. She looked at Julian with a stern aggravated look.

"Julian darling," the woman said. She outstretched a finger and curled it towards him as if to beckon him in closer.

"Marisol, I see you are out enjoying the festivities."

"Always."

"Devin, this is Marisol, an old old old friend."

She shot a look at Julian, slightly offended by the second old in the introduction. Very angry by the third.

"Enchanted," Marisol said, quickly popping herself out of an aggressive phase. She held out her hand.

Devin shook her it quickly and limply. It was damp.

She wore a long draping gray blue velvet dress. It had an aged look and she smelled a hint of mothballs. Must be for authenticity. It was as gothic as gothic could be. Must be from a thrift store.

There was a time when Devin shopped the thrift stores too. Running her fingers along the racks and boxes was magical. Each new acquisition was another puzzle piece into her new life. She met a good friend who worked at one of those stores. A cashier named Violet. Her hair was purple and her life story was tragic. For a while, she was Devin's only real friend outside of her every day world.

Marisol reminded her of Violet, except everything about Marisol was darker, blacker, and more frightening.

"Bringing friends to the party, eh?" Marisol asked Julian.

"Not this time. Not tonight."

"Pity." Marisol looked at Devin with a pouting red lip. "Why not stay and we can have some fun?"

She twirled her long white fingers through her hair. It was long dark midnight black with a streak of white blond singing out the front. She had a small ring through her lip that broke her bright blood red lipstick. Her eyes were frighteningly green.

She made Devin uncomfortable. Made her feel small. She really should have dressed better. She felt so out of place. So eager to leave.

"Actually, we were just getting ready to leave," Devin said. She nodded at Julian and started to turn around. Taking a page from Baxter's tells, she kept a stern face. Stoic.

This is like a crazy Halloween party and she forgot her costume. She felt so out of place and on display.

Breathe Devin.

Marisol reached out and grabbed Devin's wrist. It jolted her from her turn. She twisted to get out of her grasp. Devin was stronger than she looked. She shook free. Marisol looked surprised. That is what ten years of forced ballet gets you, plus kickboxing with her brother Joe. She fought dirty when she had to. She felt with Marisol, she might have to.

Devin pushed opened the ballroom door and stepped out into the hallway. She walked briskly down the stained mauve and flowered corridor. The air breezed around her. This time it was warm not cool. The stuffy dead air of a hotel ventilation system.

"Why must you always interfere?" Julian hissed at Marisol.

"With a history like ours, how can you stay away? You know how badly you want to see me. I can always tell Julian. You hide your feelings poorly."

She leaned in and ran her fingers down his chest. The heat between them was palatable.

He stood it for a few seconds and then pushed her back.

"Not now. Not anymore," he turned and walked away from her, after Devin.

Marisol hissed curse words underneath her breath and disappeared back into the crowd of partygoers.

Julian pushed the door open hard with both fists.

BANG! BANG!

"Devin stop!"

"What the hell for?"

He jogged ahead a few steps to meet up with her lead. His breath staggered. Breathless. Maybe Marisol had sucked all the passion right out of him.

Surprising.

"What happened?" he asked. "I thought it would be…a good idea for you to meet some people…before we got down to the hard facts about vampires…besides, you looked like you could use…a fun night out."

She stopped sharply and cut him an angry look.

"A fun night out? How dar…." she began to say, pausing feeling the rise of embarrassment inside.

How could he tell? How did he know? It had been months since she last went out with friends and even longer since she went out with a man.

Julian is a man. She smelled it on him.

His sharp features curled along his face. His frustration obvious. His realization of her secrets, apparent.

"Well, an entertaining adventure, how about that?" he said. "You are too detached from this subject matter. You need to learn the book facts, but come on, you need to get some excitement about the subject. I'm trying to bring you in closer."

"Closer?!"

He raised his right hand and slowly placed it on her shoulder. He pressed weight down with his hand and she felt immobile.

Her breathing slowed, as did his. Somehow he could calm her down just right.

"Maybe I rushed you."

"You didn't rush me. I just think this stuff is stupid."

"Maybe I underestimated you."

He removed his hand from her shoulder and crossed both of them in front of his chest. It reminded her of Baxter's usual teacher pose.

"Let's just get to the facts and get out of this freak show."

"Maybe we just need to sit down and have a nice long chat about how to accurately portray vampires. Maybe someone just needs to teach you a little bit about respect. Be thankful for help in authenticity."

Accuracy, she thought. A woman walked down the hall towards her wearing black velvet stretch pants and a black lace pirate top and sporting some really poor quality plastic vampire fangs. Fake blood dribbled down her cheek and she walked with a faux overly dramatic stride. Is this what he meant?

Authentic. Right.

Chapter Four

Devin took off walking briskly through the lobby. She felt as if she didn't leave this hotel, she would just burst inside. She longed for the quiet solitude of her large loft apartment, where she knew every echo like the back of her hand. It was safe there. Safe when she was alone. When she could scream when she needed to and cry when she needed to. Where she didn't have to run.

Julian followed behind her quickly. The sound of his boots hitting the ground rang in the hallway.

Devin could hear him coming closer by the second. She grew more and more irritated with every boot stomp.

Why doesn't he just leave me alone?

"Devin, where are you going?"

"I'm leaving right now."

"Stop for a minute."

She stopped short and huffed out a puff of air. Her arms flailed out besides her in a motion of giving up. She at least owed him a short explanation.

"This is silly. I'm calling for a cab. I don't need any of this. I'm leaving."

"No, you're not," he said with a stern commanding tone, reaching out and grabbing her hand.

"I can figure all this crap out for myself. I don't need you to cart me around to freak shows with your weird ass friends".

She could not twist herself from his grasp. It was hard and strong. Stronger than Marisol's. She gave in to it only because she had to.

"Come on, give it a little more time please. I need you to do this. I need you here."

In a second his demeanor changed. His words softened like those in Devin's romance novels. Each letter dripped with sex and desperation. He laid her hand against his chest.

She spread out her fingers and listened for his heartbeat.

"Me? You need me? What the hell for? Baxter hired you to help me. Or did you just forget that?"

"Oh, so that's how it is?" he said. "I'm the help. I thought that we were going to work on this together. Help each other. I thought we could learn from each other, but I guess you're too good for that."

Devin turned slowly around away from Julian with her mouth slightly pouted open in shock. No one ever talked to her in that tone. She was the boss. She always somehow became the boss, except with Baxter. She needed to be the boss in this situation.

Julian challenged her.

She liked it. She hated it.

"This is my writing assignment Julian. It all rests on my head. I'm in charge of it."

"I thought Baxter was in charge."

Arrogant asshole. Baxter too. The two of them make a great pair.

"It's my book. Did you forget that? I don't need any help. I'll do just fine on my own thank you very much. I always have written solo."

She slid her hand off his chest and crossed her arms in front of her. Very standoff-ish. This conversation would end on her terms.

Julian let out a heavy sigh. He paused and waited a few seconds for Devin too cool down. He needed her to re-think this whole partnership.

"Let's go upstairs and talk," he said gesturing towards the elevator. "It's quiet and we can be alone."

"Wha…hold. I don't know what you think, but I never agreed to *that* kind of help."

She held her hands up in the air as if to push him back.

"That's not what I meant. Ok. I have a room. We can talk about the book. Settle down. Ok? We both need this Dev."

She paused for a moment and then in a sigh of defeat, puffed out the air in her lungs and nodded her head. She knew she needed these facts and it killed her. She stepped forward and followed his lead. She wouldn't let him know why. Somehow she felt close to him. Very close.

No one called her Dev, but her father.

They quietly stepped onto the awaiting elevator. It closed with only two passengers.

The trip upstairs was in silence, as was the walk down the hall. The quiet or white noise of the hallway was deafening. She was certain Julian could hear her heart pounding anxiously in her chest. Being alone with any man made her nerves tick. Even when that man was Baxter. Especially, when that man was any other man in the world besides Baxter.

The door to the room eased open with a slow creak. It didn't seem to be locked. It took a few minutes for Devin's eyes to adjust.

Julian breezed right into the near darkness. It was dimly lit by one small table lamp. He said it was his room, but Devin doubted him as soon as she stepped through the door. A light blue coat hung loosely over a large burnt red armchair. Julian slid his hand over the top of the chair and made the coat disappear into the darkness of the floor. Small items were scattered on the dresser. A large old coin, some sort of lip gloss, a pen, used tissues, a folder piece of notebook paper, and a woman's hairbrush. The whole room smelled of perfume.

Curious.

He pulled the chair out from the wall and faced it towards the bed. He gestured with his right hand for her to sit.

Reluctantly, she sauntered over to the bed's edge and sat down exhaling a large huff. The flowered bedspread aired out around her frame as she sat. She shuffled nervously into a comfortable position. Her eyes finally adjusting. She had a chance to take in the rest of the room.

There was a small desk in one corner with a black lamp sitting atop and heavy dark curtains that shut out the world outside. The soft hum of the air conditioner buzzed from beneath the windowsill. Always too cold.

Julian reached into his coat pocket and removed a book. He tossed it down hard on the table. He brushed aside his long black coat with a sweep and sat firmly on the chair. He leaned in just inches from Devin.

She felt his hot breath on her face. Her mind was puddled with her distaste for the results of the day, her embarrassment, and the draw she felt to him with a comfort her father once gave her. She hated herself for longing to know more.

"Devin, I brought you to this convention to show you two sides of the world you need to portray in your book."

His face calmed, as did the pacing of her heartbeat.

"One side is the fan side. *Buffy* has a huge cut following that is dedicated to the core, as do many of the major sci-fi shows out there. You needed to see who your target audience is. You need to know the characters inside and out. You need to feel their pain and love their love."

That is what made her worried. The facts need to be dead on or the fans will know. That is crucial. Details about the characters and the episodes. Names, faces, worlds that were so in depth, she would never be able to fake it. How was she going to fake it? How was she going to do it without him?

"The fan side. That's one thing Julian. What is the other?"

"The second thing I wanted to show you was the darker realer side of what they crave. The mystery, the fantasy, the obsession. The mythology of the vampire, both the real and the fantasy."

"Real?"

"Yes. The real side of vampires."

"You mean Goths like Marisol?"

"Yes, Marisol," he said with a heavy breath. "But she is not here as a fan of any of these shows. She is living what they play act. She is here tonight, to hunt. To survive. To hunt among what she sees as the cattle of her cult worshippers."

"What? Because she is a real old school Goth chic? That makes her special or something?"

"No, because she is a real vampire. She is the waiting living death that they crave. She is the truth. As am I."

What did he just say?

A thick-aired silence hung in the room for at least a full minute. Devin heard her watch hands slowly *tick*, she felt the hanging humidity in the air from the hot words Julian spilled from his lips, she squinted her brow with disbelief. It grew warmer. That familiar cold breeze dissipated. Her head swam. She felt drown within it.

"You're a vampire?" she said slowly coming back to reality.

With every inch of her trying to hold back a muted chuckle under her breath. It soon gave way to a full boat of laughter, as she tilted her head back and inhaled deeply.

"Oooo, you're a vampire."

She leaned in towards him. She opened her mouth and hissed as if she had fangs and held up her hands mocking claws, lurching towards him.

"I'm soooo scared I don't know what to do. Are you gonna bite me?"

"Long before us there have been vampire stories. Hundreds, if not thousands of years of stories. The word was very old. We are not. The name soon was adopted by us. It made literal the truth of us. It gave our curse a name."

Devin's face cocked slightly to the left. A loose curl dropped in her eye and was left unattended. She was confused.

Julian allowed her to wallow in her disbelief for a moment until his patience wore thin. He needed her to listen and to understand. He needed her to believe him this instance. There was only one way to do that.

"This is ridiculous. You're a vampire? You dragged me to this stupid convention to tell me that you're a vampire! I don't know what you think of me, but I'm not that gullible. Is this some sort of sick ruse to get me into bed?"

"No. That would never be the case ever. Just listen to me…"

"Forget it. I'm leaving."

Devin made a movement to stand up, but was pushed back down on the bed by Julian's rough hand. It stung a bit and she shifted nervously. What did he want from her if not…?

He took in a deep breath, stretched his neck, and gave a slow shake to his head from left to right. It seemed as if he moved in slow motion.

This is the right choice, he thought.

As he exhaled that inhaled air, a swollen redness flushed his cheeks and his teeth dropped like pearls from his wet lips. Fangs and long ones. His expression turned from calm to intense on a dime.

Devin froze and looked at him.

"We chose to call ourselves vampires. It came eventually, as any name would come. And the very oldest, the elders, the oldest of us are called the originally cursed. I am one of those."

His eyes swallowed her laughter and below his lids it looked like pools that swam endlessly.

She saw his hunger and drank in the hot air and swallowed hard. Her throat was so dry. How desperately she needed a drink.

"Do you believe me now?"

"I…how did you? No…it can't"

He had to make her understand. He had to make her believe him, but how? Without doing something he would surely regret.

This is the right choice, he thought.

His right arm jolted out fast and grabbed her throat. It dropped any further words from struggling their way out of her mouth. His hand was large and his skin felt hard and calloused to the touch. It slowly gripped tighter with each passing second.

She let out a small squeak. The air pulled from her lips. She could barely breathe.

"Julian…stop."

He pulled her face close to his and held her there.

She felt his lust, his absolute hunger, his passion. She smelled a sickly sweet smell that reminded her of simmering citrus potpourri with a hot metallic burn underneath.

"How far do I need to go to make you listen to me?" he spit from between clenched teeth. His manner was cold and angry. "You must get past this impish naiveté, so I may show you the truth. Only then, will you have the smallest clue about what we are and how you must portray us in your book, both as truth of legacy and as a warning. It is vital that you understand the truth.

Then, I hope, you will repay my favor in kind, as I will always be true to my owes."

Devin gasped and tried to inhale his exhaled breath. It was dry and old. Like death and sex. Her head swam and she felt faint. She struggled to regain consciousness.

His face continued to pulse with intensity and now hunger. He pushed her back onto the bed, releasing his grip and sitting back in his chair, upright and solemn, in the face she had known before. The human face. He recovered quickly.

She could not recover so quickly. She flipped on the mattress like a dead fish and forced herself to sit up as quickly as possible. Mostly out of fear and dark curiosity. Her heart beat feverishly fast in her chest. She raised her left hand as if to hold it inside. Her vision was doubled. None of this made any sense.

Were those fangs plastic?

Julian just stared at her.

Is this his pitch for the book?

There was a solid ringing in her ears. The air-conditioner buzzed so loudly and the shuffle of people in the hall rose and fell every minute or so. It made her nervous, so much more nervous than anything else. She could not bear to bring anyone else into this nightmare. She also could not bear being in it alone.

"Are you ready to listen Devin?"

It caught her out of her dream stance. She stared at him a full minute in silence. Her head spun inside her skull. The possibilities, one after the other banging together in confusion.

How did he do that? What were those fangs made of? What does he really want from her? Why is she here?

His lips were wet and his teeth blindingly white. His cheeks glowed and glistened as a single droplet of sweat ran slowly down his forehead. It seemed to move just as slow as the reluctantly slowing of her heartbeat.

Devin could not get her fixated eyes off it.

"Well, Devin are you ready?"

"I…am…ready."

Chapter Five

Devin settled comfortably into the softness of the mattress. She held a pillow on her lap in subtle protection from another attack. Her fingers dug deeply into the down.

Julian reached into his coat pocket and pulled out a cigarette. He flicked the top of a Zippo lighter and the flame glowed brightly in the dark room. He took a drag on the cigarette. A crackling sound broke the dead silence.

Devin knew this would take a while.

He exhaled slowly, letting the smoke peel from his lips and curve up towards the stucco ceiling. It made amazing circles that he followed with his eyes. After a few seconds of watching he slowly began to speak.

"I was born in France. My parents were poor trades people, my father a shoemaker and my mother a seamstress. The best I could hope for in life was to garner enough education to be capable of learning a similar trade, to find a suitable wife, and make a small pittance of money to feed my children."

Devin could relate to being very middleclass. Even lower middleclass. Everything was just out of reach.

"My mother and father had survived the bitter ravage of illness that took my sister and much of Europe. It had been a difficult time, but we survived."

"What illness?" Devin wondered. Hunger? Malaria?

"The plague."

The plague? There haven't been any real plagues in her lifetime. Small outbreaks in third world countries, but not somewhere like France.

She bit her lip in an effort to hold back the questions she had. Maybe there had been a recent plague that she knew nothing about. She did not want her ignorance to be obvious. With the strange hours she kept, she often missed the nightly news and rarely bought a newspaper. Fashion magazines aside, she was not very current.

"Now with the risks of war encroaching on our small village, we chose to flee and cross the ocean to Canada. We spoke only French and hoped to find a peaceable new replacement for the life we knew."

"Wait, what war? We were just on the plague."

"At the time, I was just 22 when we arrived just outside Ralston, Alberta. It was 1940, just after the fall of France to the emerging demonish Nazis. The world was fast becoming a frightening place."

"Wait, wait World War II? Do you think I'm stupid?" Devin stopped him abruptly, holding out a hand open in front of her.

The silence had definitely been broken.

"1940? That would make you..." she counted the years silently in her head.

"Yes," he answered halting her train of thought. "Very very very old."

"But, that's not possible. You look so young. You are young."

She cocked her head slightly to the side and pouted her lips to respond, but stopped and settled back into a rested seat. She looked into Julian's eyes and felt a confused belief wash over her. The plague, World War II, this was crazy. Why did she believe him?

"We do age, unlike many vampire myths I am sure you've read. We age, just very slowly. Our bodies regenerate at a rate that yours cannot. Cells heal, wounds disappear, faster than yours would. In a way, everything about us is very young, but very old."

What a pitch, she thought. *This must be his idea for the vampire book. Wait, did he want to co-write? His name and Dena's on the cover and her name buried in the invisible lines beneath. That is so not fair.*

"I tried to settle into a normal life, forgetting the France I knew was slowing dying and tried to learn to love the new France that we were trapped in. My parents' secured jobs similar to those they had and I secured work as a cleaner in a small medical facility."

Julian shifted in his seat and reached into his coat pocket for another cigarette.

"For months I scrubbed floors and tried to acclimate myself to the life I now was forced into, until one day I felt like I awoke."

The flame of the lighter burst in front of Julian's face. His eyes glowed as he pulled on the cigarette with his lips. The soft crackling sound seemed so incredibly loud. He snapped the Zippo lighter shut with a click. Smoking must be his tell when he is nervous or serious. Devin made a mental note.

"What happened to awaken you?"

"I was in the hallway cleaning the floors when a beautiful creature slipped past me. The ripe rain scent of her perfume intoxicated me. I was drowning in fresh fallen raindrops, a hint of melon, and rawness that I had never experienced before."

Julian's face began to glow. He almost looked human.

"This beautiful creature, she turned to face me, smiled bashfully, and said *bon jour*. I was in love at that moment."

"What was her name?"

"Marguerite. Beautiful Marguerite. She was tall and slim with small curves and fair skin. Her golden brown hair tossed in loose curls against her small shoulders. Her eyes were pale like the daylight ocean waters I watched for so many days as we came from our old home to Canada. She spoke gently like the breeze and I swallowed each word like pure oxygen."

It was clear that he loved her very much. A sense of utter devotion seemed to permeate his skin and enter the air around them.

"I was a simple, uneducated cleaner and she was a scientist. At first, I thought I wouldn't have a chance with her. She went to the best schools in France and moved to Canada a few years before we did, with her sister and brother. He parents had died years prior. She shied away from telling me the details of their loss, but in her eyes I could see that it killed a part of her."

Julian leaned back in his chair and took a drag of his cigarette.

"She made me feel like a man. Less than a year after she first passed me in the hallway, she would be my wife. I felt though, that she was my soulmate from the moment our eyes first met."

Devin settled further into the soft pillow of the mattress. Her legs crossed. In this pose she waited for the story to peel itself into either a killer book idea neatly veiled by good acting or something entirely new in this world.

"We lived in a small apartment. We had a simple but wonderful life."

Julian stopped speaking for a second and looked down at the carpeted floor between his knees. The intensity of the love he felt for his wife was coming off him in waves. A single tear rolled its way down his cheek and splashed against the dark floor.

Devin reached out towards him with her left hand and softly placed it on his shoulder. He did not flinch. They sat motionless like that for several minutes. Devin thought about what he had told her so far. There was some very real and dark truth in this book idea of his. The words he spoke seemed unreal and impossible, but the sadness in his eyes combined with the very real image of white pearls glistening deadly between his lips, forced her to at least hear him out. She felt so confused. Trapped between the story and the reality of what she had just seen. Although, costuming and such had advanced so far. They *must* have been plastic fangs.

Suddenly, Julian stood up to the sound of a soft *thump thump* echoing in the quiet room.

Devin could not tell where exactly it had come from.

Julian excused himself and slipped into the bathroom. He looked down at the pale face of a frightened woman. Reclaiming his vampire face, he sunk his long white fangs deeply into her neck. She struggled, but was bound and gagged on the bathroom floor and unable to move much. His eyes spun wildly as the blood ran its way down his hot throat. A few muffled minutes later, he returned to Devin by the bed. He felt confident he had hidden the sound of the body dropping into the bathtub. A small drop of blood sat in the corner of his mouth. He lapped at it like a hungry dog. Hiding the crime he had committed to garner the use of the room, but now he was energized and could continue his conversation with Devin more comfortably.

Devin pretended not to notice as he sat back down in the chair before her. *Just a story. Just a book idea. Just her imagination. There was no one.* She convinced herself. She leaned in towards him and coaxed the story forward. She felt intoxicated by him. Blind to what ever else may be going on around her.

"What happened to her Julian? What happened to your wife?" seeing that the look in his eyes as his head rose up held a terrible truth.

"Not a year after we were wed, Marguerite's work changed significantly."

He raised his hand to his lips to take one last drag on his cigarette. Then, he dropped it effortlessly towards the ground, where a glass of water sat waiting in the darkness.

"The government scientists believed that their livestock was very susceptible to many vicious old world diseases. They feared that some of these diseases could be transmitted to humans. Marguerite's research was meant to save the lives of humans and cattle alike."

"That sounds very noble."

"It was. While looking to protect themselves and create vaccines, they also began to be heavily influenced by the increasing military concerns the world over. This was war time remember. People were scared out of their minds. They looked high and low for an answer that could save them. They were looking for ways to introduce these diseases that possible could be transmitted to humans, while making sure they had all antidotes in place for themselves."

"You mean like biological warfare?" Devin asked.

"I guess, but that was before anyone really named it. It was just darkness then."

"Darkness is a good name for it."

"Marguerite's research team had been working on the vaccines. The entire world was teetering on the edge of a horrific possible future. It was 1942 and England sent a group of scientists to Alberta to assist."

"I never remember hearing about that."

"The Brits had been working on several chemical weapons. One year earlier, they disseminated anthrax spores from small aircraft bombs off the coast of Scotland at Gruinard Island. Most of their work was so classified that Marguerite did not even know the results, but I know to this very day, that island is uninhabitable."

"So they already knew when they arrived that they had something potentially deadly and they brought it with them anyway?" Devin said.

"Yes they did. The military had all but taken over. Chemical weapons, biological weapons, fear, money, and the emerging ignorance of a mid-20th century low-tech science world. This was a dangerous mixture. Add in everyone's huge egos and it was unbearable."

It sounded like a recipe for disaster.

"What about Marguerite?"

"Marguerite, I'm not sure how, but she changed into someone else. Her work consumed her. They forced it into her, but she also loved the idea that she could be a part of a bigger global solution. They began experimenting with various physically crippling diseases. They wanted to find something that disfigured, but did not kill. They tested these horrors on the livestock. Blood oozed from their pores and their flesh wilted like the leaves of dead plants."

His hand dropped forward mimicking the imaging of a plant wilting. His fingers were long and pale, like his face. The hands of an old man trapped in a young man's body. Full of calluses and wisdom.

Devin cringed from the terrible image Julian scripted. It made her sick, but at the same time, she wondered if this *was* a book idea or better yet, a movie idea, how cool the special effects could be.

"One of the scientists on Marguerite's team was working on a little known disease. He wanted to find a vaccine, but also find a way to transmit the disease, if need be. He came up with the idea of Porphyria after working with the livestock."

"What is Porphyria?"

"A tragic human disease. It primarily affect the skin, causing sensitivity to sunlight, blisters, and necrosis of the skin and gums. The urine, teeth, and fingernails can turn reddish brown. It is a terrible sight to see."

"It sounds terrible."

Devin knew that he did see it somehow. They must have been successful in cursing someone with this disease. His eyes told a matter of fact story.

"It is what many authors throughout time have fabled as *the vampire disease* and that people in years past were so naïve and so young in their understanding of the universe, that they blamed things they could not understand on vampires. Those cursed with Porphyia, gave them flesh and blood villains to blame."

"*That* I have heard before somewhere."

Devin thought about a show she once saw on a health TV channel. She remembered the reference to vampires as part of the curse of this disease. It belittled the condition, but also held some real truth for those who did not know any better. Today is one thing, but World War II was something entirely different. A different time.

"What happened with their research Julian?"

"Gale, Broda, and Katia happened. The British scientists that had been sent over from England to help Marguerite's research team. They had arrived under the falsity that they would help with the weapons research."

Julian fidgeted in his seat uncomfortably. Something about mentioning their names made him nervous. He grabbed his lighter and began twirling it between his calloused fingertips. The *click click* sound of the top was like a nervous tick.

"By the time their true motives were uncovered, it was too late. They were Nazi spies. They tried to steal Marguerite's team's research. A terrible fight ensued. The lab was a mess with spilled chemicals everywhere. They were all exposed, the scientists. Seven of them and me."

"You got sick? Exposed to Porphyria?"

"A transmittable mutated version of it yes. A stronger and more deadly version that Marguerite's team had created."

Julian let out a large sigh. It was as if talking about what happened allowed a huge weight to be lifted from his shoulders. It must have been years since he spoke with someone so honestly.

"After we got sick, Marguerite and I went and stayed at my parent's home. They and Marguerite's brother cared for us in secrecy. I…it was really bad. The others, they took similar refuge."

Devin could see that this was very difficult for him to talk about. His own suffering.

"Tell me about them. The others."

"Marguerite's research team consisted of her and two other Canadian scientists. Plus, a research assistant. Maks was the lead scientist. He had been at the facility for years longer than anyone else. He was deeply into all his research. He isolated himself from the others. He was short and unusual looking. I personally never really got along with him."

"Why not?"

"As strong as I have always been, he even scared me."

"You...scared?"

"Don't look so surprised. I was *only human* then."

Devin chuckled, but the thought of him being not human made her a little tense. What did that make him? A monster?

"Did he die? You refer to him in the past tense."

"We all were exposed to the Porphyria modified strain. But we didn't know it yet. At first we just thought we were sick, not dying. It took several weeks for the full effect to become apparent. He became a vampire, just like me. One of the originally cursed ones."

"And now?"

"No one really knows. He isolated himself for so long."

"And the others?"

"The other Canadian scientist, beside Marguerite, was named Danica. Danica Southerlyn."

"Is she dead now?"

"In a way, we all are dead now Dev."

"I guess it is a hard concept for me to understand."

"Danica was a good scientist, but an even better manipulator. She was lean, athletic, and attractive with short dark hair. She could get men and even some women to do whatever she wanted them to do. Then, leave them crushed."

Julian stood up and walked over to the window. He slowly slid a portion of the heavy curtain open and stared out into the darkness of the night. He seemed somewhat upset speaking about Danica. Devin wondered if maybe they had been friends.

"Is she around still Julian?"

"Maybe. She moves around a lot. Taking what she can from people. Living off their good fortune. Most lose their life for it."

There was real pity in his eyes. This was a reality that he had come to accept. There will be deaths. Lots of deaths to keep all of them *alive*.

"So, Marguerite was the third scientist? On the project?"

"Yes. She, Danica, and Maks really began with good intentions. They were true humanitarian scientists, all of them. They would have ended with good intentions, had the others not arrived. Damn them!"

Julian turned back around from the window. His face now had a streak of anger. Devin knew that if he had the chance he would kill Gale, Broda, and Katia.

"They also hired a research assistant in preparation for the scientists coming from England. His name was Macan. François Macan. Now he, well he is a whole different story."

Devin was curious. Julian's eyes had a strange glow now as he stood in front of the window. There must be something really interesting about this Macan guy. Why did that name sound so familiar?

"Tell me about him. Tell me about Macan."

"He was gorgeous. All the women wanted him. The men wanted to look like him. Dark hair, smoldering dark eyes, striking sharp features. He was young, so young back then.

Recently out of college, eager to learn, to please. Marguerite looked after him, like a younger brother."

There was something unbearable in Julian's eyes.

"You cared for him too, didn't you?"

"When we began to get sick. It was very bad. We were all bed bound, being cared for by family members. The military was worried that the public would find out about the outbreak, so they would not allow us to go to regular doctors or regular hospitals. Their doctors stopped by sometimes, but could do no more than give us pain pills. Macan abandoned science all together. Refused treatment."

"What happened to him?"

"He isolated himself. We found out much later that he really lost himself in the head. Some say insane, I say eccentric. He played the violin, self-taught and genius. Played for us when we were still bedridden. For a while, later on, I lived near him in a small village outside Rome. Late at night, you could hear the song of the violin cursing the darkness with sad yet fierce music."

"Is he still there? In Rome?"

"No. He is here. He still plays the violin, but has really made a big name for himself in the art world as a painter."

"Art world?" Devin said with a bit of trepidation.

"A painter. Dark macabre paintings. Oil and blood. Only the buyers don't know about the blood."

Julian walked slowly up to Devin, where she sat on the edge of the bed. He leaned forward and looked her in the eyes closely.

"You have one of his paintings in your living room. The picture of the cat surrounded by dead leaves and roses."

She loved that painting. She made the connection. She had instantly been drawn to it when she saw it in that downtown chic art gallery. It drew her in. Maybe some unconscious part of her knew. Smelled the blood mixing with the oil paint. Maybe she saw some ugly face that called to her. But, how did Julian know about the painting? Unless he had been in her apartment, there was no way for him to know. Maybe those prying eyes of the city that she feels watching her, really do watch her.

"How did you…"

"Know about the painting? I know you Devin. Make no mistake."

"But, it makes no…"

"I *know* you Devin," Julian stressed and told her without words that this part of the conversation was off limits for now.

Devin rolled her eyes up to meet Julian's. She knew he was not going to tell her anything else about how he knew about the painting. She was almost afraid to ask anymore.

"Ok…so, about Macan then."

"He rarely shows himself, except at the occasional late night gallery showing. Mostly, he just fucks and feeds his way through the art world. Oil and blood. Oil and blood and more blood."

Her head was spinning with the details of this crazy story. A lump in her throat tried to halt the words that she needed to spill from her lips.

God, it's dry in this room.

"Macan, I never met him. The painting just…"

"Drew you in? You can recognize us, you know. You feel me coming, don't you?"

"I don't know. Maybe I do."

"Do you feel a strange sensation? A cold chill perhaps?"

"Yes…the cool breeze."

"Your sense must be so strong that you could even feel it calling you through the painting. That is amazing and can prove to be very useful to you."

Devin remembers seeing the painting hanging on a lone wall at the gallery. Everyone else that looked at it seemed disturbed, but she was enthralled. She left that night with it in her arms.

"Macan rounded out the Canadian science team. Then came…the others. Gale, Broda, and Katia. At first, they were simply inquisitive and helpful. Later we learned that they were not in fact the scientists we thought they were. They were spies who had murdered the scientists that were supposed to come and help Marguerite's team. Vicious and deadly. Katia died right after we were all infected. She is in fact, the only original that I know for sure to be dead."

"How did she die?"

"Gale and Broda, at least those are the names we knew them by. At this point, who really knows who they are? They killed her for betraying the fatherland. Their violence is legendary."

"Tell me what they were like Julian."

"Gale was tall and chiseled like a Greek statue. His stoic expression. He was perfection in every way. Everyone wanted him. Men, women, but Broda most of all. The passion between them was palatable."

"They were lovers?"

"Almost more than that. Broda completed him and vice versa. She was blond with flowing curls and piercing blue eyes. The perfect picture of their Arian perfection. I was the least surprised to discover that they were Nazi spies. Physical perfection and a totality in evil."

Something about Julian's description of Gale and Broda frightened Devin more so that the others. They were evil as regular humans, so that must make them super evil in death. The thought of meeting them sent a chill down her back. She shuddered on the bed. Her pillow griped tightly between her fingers.

Julian lit another cigarette. The room hung in heavy silence. The only sound was his inhalation and exhalation. The twisted smoke curling upwards towards the ceiling. He almost looked a bit frightened himself.

"Are they around…here?"

"Always. I believe right now they own a small chain of restaurants, but they always have an ulterior motive. They are not simply cuisine aficionados. I don't know what it is now, but I know it must be bad."

"The one spy, the one they killed, how did or could she die? I thought vampires couldn't die easily."

"A good axe to the neck will bring anyone down." Julian said as he ran his finger across his throat in a slicing motion.

"They say that they cut her up and fed her to their restaurant patrons. No one knows for sure, but I wouldn't be surprised."

"Ugh! People stew," Devin shivers.

She began to see that it was not like the movies. No vampires turning into a puff of smoke or a bat. No super human powers to fly or withstand any injury. No lack of reflections in the mirror and long black flowing capes.

"We have no idea what affect that could have on the humans that may have eaten her. Maybe worse that what we suffer with everyday."

There was now fear and sadness in Julian's eyes. He was suffering. Loosing Marguerite, living this unlife, the painful legacy of his cursed brethren, the responsibility he feels for them and their actions. He let it rest heavy on his shoulders all these years. He was now ready to relieve some of that burden.

"Have you ever tried to stop them?"

"It's complicated. There are rules that I have not always been able to abide by, but now with you at my side, maybe we can do something."

"Me? What can I do? I'm just a writer and not even a very good one at that. There is nothing I could do to help you fight vampires."

"You, in your faithfulness and humanity can help lead me to the no longer human. To end them. To bring Marguerite home to me."

"Then what? After you bring her home, then what?"

Julian didn't answer.

"I...you need to understand Julian, I have never been a fighter. I don't know how I could possibly be of any help to you. It sounds like you need warriors and I can tell you for sure, I'm not one."

"I am not looking for a warrior. I am looking for a guide. I just need to get close and you can help me."

Without another word, Devin just knew. After all this time and all that had happened to him, Julian was not just looking for a guide. He was looking for a hunter.

Chapter Six

What a strange and unique story Julian was scripting. Maybe Devin could use some of it in her new book for Baxter. She still could not explain the fact that in some small dark way, she believed this all to be true. She also still could not explain those fangs. She opted to keep going, real or not, she could not stop listening.

"How sick did you get Julian?"

"We had terrible wounds that bled and seeped. We were exhausted, dehydrated, and pale. Our skin was so dry. Our gums receded. We had a hunger that could not be quenched. The hunger was…is unbearable."

Devin shivered. She was not sure if it was from the image in her head or the cool breeze that seemed to follow her everywhere she went.

"These family members of ours soon became our nurses and caretakers. Bathing us, treating our wounds, bringing our meals, closing the curtains to shut out the painful sunlight."

Julian blinked from imaginary bright light and by habit raised the back of his hand to his eyes and squinted.

"What bothered you about sunlight?"

"We became super sensitive to it. I don't know why, but it burned our skin like the worst sunburn you can imagine. So bad it bled."

Devin cringed, remembering sunburns in her past. She could still feel the hot pain stinging her skin. It was like a thousand tiny razor blades making their way across the continent of her back.

"This went on for months. Our caretakers were nicknamed commerçants de sang or blood traders. Their trade had become to care for those…bloodied."

Devin could imagine the gruesome image in her head. She had watched many a show on the health and surgery channels, but seeing Julian's face made it too real. She could actually see him disfigured and bloody.

"After some time, the wounds began to heal. Our physical outsides grew back to health, but inside, we were different. We craved blood."

"Vampires? You became like vampires?" Devin asked him.

"We *were* vampires. Maybe the first real ones. Who knows? Eventually, we all turned on our relatives and fed. We all became very very ill. Marguerite and the other scientists surmised that the blood of our relatives, our same bloodline, was poison to us. A little just made us sick, but a full draining would kill us. The cravings were unbearable though. Soon our blood traders were caring for our new weakness and soon everyone realized that we need blood to survive."

"Vampires," Devin said in a whisper, matter of fact this time.

"Every week or so, our blood traders became our hunters. At first, it was prostitutes and homeless people. Those that no one would miss or care about. As our strength grew, we began to hunt on our own."

There was a subtle shame in Julian's eyes. This horrible curse that had been given to him like a bad cold made him do unspeakably terrible things.

"You had no choice, right?"

"The power of it was intoxicating. Soon, our blood traders became our cleaners. Now, not hunters, they needed to constantly follow behind us and clean up the messes we left behind. They felt an obligation, as family. And loving us as they did and understanding that we were sick, they kept our terrible secrets."

The shame now mixed with an undercurrent of lust. Devin could almost feel Julian's lips on her throat, drinking her, consuming her completely. She lifted her hand to her throat. She wanted it. She needed it to believe this crazy story.

"As the years went on, we noticed that we were physically healthier than those we knew. The general theory in common folklore of vampires is that vampires never aged, but the exact opposite it actually true. We regenerate and age remarkably fast. Our skin, our bones, or blood, everything was always new. Regenerated, just like your hair or nails."

"Regeneration. Amazing."

"Our loved ones grew older and died, so new family members took their place."

"Must stay the bloodline. The ones you cannot kill."

"Yes Dev. We knew that we could never feed on them, as we became terribly sick. That gave us an unspoken trust that no one could break."

Julian spoke with a solidness to his tone. That was the vampire law. That was the code of secrecy. Trust.

"As technology grew, the blood traders became more involved in business. They became our business faces in the daylight. If one vampire needed assistance with something, we bartered with services instead of the world's money. Money had no meaning anymore. It was all about the blood. We all became very reclusive. Mostly from fear. I from shame."

Julian's face drew from solid to solemn. He looked ashamed. Ashamed for a million crimes that Devin longed to know. He paused for what felt like minutes.

Devin reached out her hand and stroked his shoulder seeming to awaken him back to the dry-aired reality of the hotel room and the convention-goers just floors below. How separated Devin felt from them. They played and dressed-up this world that Julian lived in. How little they would want to if they knew the truth of it.

Finally, his head perked up. He shook off the coat of uncomfortability that surrounded him.

Content on finishing the story or plot, Devin still wondered in the back of her mind. Great storyteller.

"The remaining scientists wanted to understand the disease, maybe replicate it, maybe cure it. In those early days we learned quickly too that if we drained someone completely and they were left in a protected area, like indoors, they became like us. They went through the same illness. We infected them. We became careful not to fully drain many. To allow them to survive."

"You made new vampires."

"Just some. Those that became sick from us, could not pass the disease along. Those they drained seemed immune."

"How is that possible?"

"The disease mutates as soon as we pass it along. That next strain cannot be transmitted. Only death comes to those."

"So the people you drank from, they just became vampires right? You never killed anyone," Devin hilted a question mark at the end through the use of a higher octave.

"I killed," he answered.

Then nothing more about that fact.

Devin knew it was the inevitability of the story. How could a vampire not kill, if they wished to survive? That was the first truth of vampire lore anywhere. Vampires kill. Vampires drink blood. Vampires are monsters, but Julian did not feel like a monster to her. He felt like a friend.

"I tried to handle the brunt of the dirty work to keep my wife sane, but Marguerite began acting more iritic. She became paranoid and started not wanting to leave the house. One night, we fought. She had been sick for days. Her face was pale and she had a hunger she could not satisfy, but also a terrible stomachache. We argued. She lashed out at me and scratched at my face. When the blood ran down my cheek, she was on me. She bit me on the shoulder and drank."

He pulled the right collar of his shirt out wide with his hand. He turned his head to the left and exposed an old faded scar along his shoulder blade. Marguerite had fed on him.

"Her teeth were so sharp, I passed out. The next thing I remember, I was on the floor and Marguerite was gone. The front door was smashed open and some of her things were missing."

"Where did she go? What happened to her?"

"They needed her. They knew it. The other scientists. She was lost to me."

"They kidnapped her?"

"They felt stronger and wanted to understand it, to use it. This new cursed power we had. But they needed Marguerite's scientific expertise. I think in some way, she went willingly."

Julian's eye sunk deeply into their sockets. His loss was profound.

"The instincts I was feeling drove me to them with a hunger I had never felt before."

"And what did you find?"

"Marguerite had chosen them over me. She left me and sought out a way to replicate the disease with the other scientists. I was alone. The two Nazis soon joined with the other scientists. I could not be a part of what they were trying to do. We were damned. We were sick and the last thing I wanted to do was to infect any more people."

"The plague," Devin whispered. This was the real plague that Julian knew, not the one that scattered its way through Europe. Only, no one knew about this one.

"A power struggle was beginning in our own secret world. Who would rule and command over the new rising covens out there? There needed to be rule, but by whose hand was the problem."

Julian stopped speaking for a minute and stood up. He slowly walked over to the window and billowed open the heavy curtains. He stared out into the eyes of the nighttime city like a lost child. Devin knew he looked for only Marguerite. She wondered if somewhere, she was looking for him.

"10 years had passed since the accident, the infection. They had moved as a group into the states and settled, just outside the Chicago. I followed them down but was kept apart from them. My father had been my blood trader and he passed away. The others would not do any business with me without one. I was isolated and alone."

Devin could feel his loneliness. She imagined it had been years since he had been able to talk to anyone as he talked to her. Wait. Reality girl. This cannot be real.

He slowly turned back around and looked to her as if for guidance.

"Go on Julian. Tell more of the *story*."

A soft grin appeared on her face.

Julian was noticeably irritated.

"I tried to find her, to get access to her. I had hoped that if we saw each other that she would have a change of heart. I felt guilt and hoped she would come to me. She never did."

It was clear in his face that he still waited for her each night. Something unconscious still believed that she would come.

"You still loved her."

"I did. Then my attitude changed. One night, when I awoke, I was being hit in the face with a pipe. It was Gale. The last thing I remember was the smile on Marguerite's face and the light flicker of her laughter out of the corner of my left eye, as I was knocked unconscious. She took every piece of research we had hidden away."

"Did she know how to re-create the virus?"

"No. No one knew exactly. However, from that moment on I knew that I had to take responsibility for the others. I knew that as much as I loved Marguarite, that I needed to end it. I could not allow her and the others to recreate the disease, to infect others. We all just needed to die out. Then no new vampires would be cursed, as we were."

"You wanted to kill them."

"Yes. They turned other scientists and doctors into vampires, each time trying and failing. I secretly watched them kill all those who failed. As time went on and medicine advanced, it became frightening that they might succeed. Then, one day I lost track of them. I could find the blood traders, but not my kind. And they would not speak to me and from that day on, I have searched for Marguerite and also for a family member. Without one, I can never enter their world and be listened to. I am isolated. I need a member of my family to help me end a silent terrible war that we helped create."

Julian stopped for a moment and stood up. He walked slowly over to the sink resting just outside the bathroom. He slowly tuned the handle on the sink and placed his left had cupped under the cold water. He brought it to his face in a splash and shook it off. He seemed to move in slow motion. He had a reflection. That was always a vampire thing that never made any sense. Why did all the vampires on TV and in the movies never have reflections? Why wouldn't they take photographs of themselves all the time to see what they looked like?

Devin could feel the heat in the room increase a couple degrees. Was she having a hot flash? A panic attack? Was Julian somehow doing it to he? Did he give her drugs? Maybe that was why she thought his face contorted earlier. Maybe this was some big kinky ploy to get her into bed. She had fallen for worse when she was younger.

When a sad story about a dead father or a lost dog would make her think a teenage boy was sensitive and that he would respect her. When she so wanted to believe that someone was her soul mate and loved her. Like a princess.

How did her slip her drugs? She stood up trying to shake off the effect.

"Julian," she said sharply "what did you *give* me?"

He slowly turned away from the sink. He looked at her with a puzzled look.

"Give you?" he asked. "What do you mean?"

"Give me. Slip me."

"You think I drugged you? Or do you mean what kind of bullshit story did I give you?" he walked back over towards her.

She felt the heat from him. It made her breath heavy and hot.

Irritation began to drip of him like the water from the sink.

"I thought we were past the proof thing Dev," getting within inches of her face.

"Proof?" she said with a solid questioning tone.

Her mind was so twisted. Half wrapped up in this intoxication she felt and half sworn on the fact that this all must be fake somehow, a lie. She tilted her head to the right. Bushing back a few loose hairs falling on her shoulder, she exposed her neck from the edge of her white blouse.

"Prove it then," she said.

She knew that this would solve it. Make it rationalized in her mind, whichever side won. If he cannot bite her, than it was fake. If he did and it was real, like a part of her longed for in the drug induced fog, then maybe it was. Either way, it would be proven. She knew he would not bite her. She knew it.

He looks down towards the floor and gives his shoulder a slow dry shrug. His head sways slowly from side to side and his temples turn cherry red again. Droplets of sweat pool up on his forehead and nose. He raises his eyes upward and looks into hers.

"Are you sure?" he asked her.

"Yes I'm sure."

Devin sees his eyes shine, like wet from tears. His long white fangs drew her in. She let out a long slow breath and waited for her answer.

His lips met her throat in a second. It felt as if he was kissing her hard. A rough passioned embrace, like the ones she wrote about in her romance novels. Steaming with some overdone fire that she had never experienced in real life, only learned how to train herself to write about.

He smelled of oranges and lemons, but warm.

She drank in the smell of him on her for a moment, until she realized there was pain. She awoke herself out of the intoxicating fog and felt that the long passionate kiss was hurting her.

"Jule…" she managed to spit out softly. "Jul…e…stop."

For what seemed like hours, Julian clutched her in that tight embrace. Drinking from her waiting throat like she bore the very fruit of life for all man. Then, he suddenly let go and allowed her to collapse on the bed below. The flowered bedspread rippled out from under the mattress as she powered down upon it, adding to the collection of fluids with stray drops of her blood.

Devin laid there for several minutes, unaware of where Julian was in the room. She could feel the two small wounds pulsing above her shoulder. There was no way that fake plastic fangs could have done that, she repeated silently in her head.

"Drugs could not do that," she whispered almost silently.

She planted her hands firming into the soft down of the bed and forced herself into a seated position. She let out a sigh and looked around for Julian.

He walked from across the room slowly, as if he had been waiting hours for her to wake up. Maybe he had been. Maybe most of this had all been a dream. A drug induced dream. He handed her a small white washcloth from the bathroom towel supply. She raised it to the wound on her neck and brought it back down. Cherry red spheres of blood soaked deep into the bleached white towel.

"It was real," she whispered a little louder this time, and now believed for certain. All doubt erased.

"For years I have been looking for just the right person to help me. Marguerite and I had one daughter that we gave to our best friend to raise after we became ill. We were terrified that we would harm her. It was the best thing for her. After my mother and father died, I sought her out and could not find her. I needed someone that knew the real world, the surface world well, but longed for another."

"Did you ever find her?"

"I found her granddaughter."

"Have you met her?"

"As soon as I saw you in Baxter's office."

Devin looked up at Julian slowly. Her faced cringed into a slight look of pain and utter confusion.

"I knew it was you."

"Knew I was what?" she asked him.

"I knew that you would understand the difference between the real world and…my world. I knew that you would come at any challenge with the fierceness that you approach your work. I need an advocate. I need someone like you to get into the heart of…my world. They all have them. Commerçants de sang, remember. Blood traders. The human faces of my kind that move in the daylight. Trusted ones. More trusted than we trust each other. They are the merchants of the dead."

"What does that have to do with your meeting me at Bax's office?" Devin asked puzzled completely at this point.

"I need you to be mine."

"Your blood trader?" she uttered with a stint of sarcasm. "Yeh, no I don't think so. No more blood. Besides, you said they needed to be family. I imagine the others would know somehow or you would have found someone else long ago."

She lifted the towel back to her throat and sighed at the stinging of the wound. Beneath the pain was an undercurrent of pleasure that she could not explain and was too embarrassed to express.

"It is more complicated than just finding anyone to be my blood trader," Julian said as he crouched down in front of her.

His eyes were even with hers and his look ran with sympathy.

"We can go out in the daylight, but only briefly. Only minutes. The affects of the sun attack us like a violent sunburn that we cannot heal from. The commerçants de sang are loyal partners with my kind. They are the daylight faces. I need one."

He exhaled and stood up straight, turning and walking slowly back towards the window. He stopped and rested his hand on the windows edge.

"They feel a loyalty and responsibility to us," he turned back around and looked at her.

"They would know Julian. They would know I am not your family. Wouldn't you if someone tried to pull that trick?"

"I thought my family was all dead. That I would never find the decedents of my daughter Claudette. Until I found you."

Devin paused short and ran through the family rolodex in her mind. Could it possibly be? She thought. No way. There is no way that her grandmother Claudette is the same Claudette that was his lost daughter. That is just insane.

"I need you to help me get close enough."

"Close enough to who?"

"To my wife. To Marguerite."

Devin and Julian sat silently in the room for what seemed like hours. He would say a few words every few minutes. It seemed as if he had to rip the words from his very soul in order to get them out. She inhaled them, letter after letter, syllable after syllable, line after line. They penetrated her very soul.

The vampires had created a very controlled and secret hierarchy. Now that only a few original ones remained and yet a handful of others they created, they needed to be very discreet in order to survive.

Each one had a commerçant de sang that was a direct family member. A loyal business partner of sorts that walked the waking world and conducted business with other commerçants de sang. It stood for blood trader and traders of blood are what they had become.

One blood trader, along with their vampire, may have the ability to dispose of bodies, while another may have a unique interest in financial markets. They traded services under the cloak of secrecy and they only did business with each other. No vampire alone could approach them. It was an affront to their dead.

"You want me to pose as your trader?" she asked him.

"Not pose, be," he answered, "I want you to be my trader. I want you to help me find Marguerite. We have both lived a long life and it is time to close this chapter."

"You want to kill her?" she spurted out accusatory.

"Yes. I wish I could say no," he said. "I want to bring us together one more time. I know that she senses what I sense. That this needs to end. We can walk out…together. Spend one last sunrise on the hill overlooking Pebble Park."

Julian's eyes teared up. He turned away to hide that fact from Devin almost ashamed of loving Marguerite so much.

Devin reached out and placed her hand on his knee. The pain from the wound on her neck was receding and she could feel just how much pain he was in. It superceded her pain by thousands.

"You have spent sixty plus years searching for her, haven't you?" she asked.

He did not respond.

"Why me?" she asked him. She could not understand why out of all the people in the world would he pick a young loser ghostwriter.

"I do love her, but I must kill her. It must be me. And it must be you. Remember how I told you that the original blood traders were family? Well, I have been searching for years for family and I finally found you."

"Me?" Devin asked stunned. "You said you needed family. I can't be your family. I just can't."

"What is your grandmother's maiden name Devin?"

"LaShrou. Why?"

"Your great grandmother, do you know anything about her?"

"No. Nothing. I think my great grandparents died just before my grandparents came to this country."

"Devin, your great grandmother is Marguerite and I am your great grandfather."

Chapter Seven

She ran through the possibility in her head, Grandma Claudette's parents were from somewhere in Europe she thought, maybe near France. She had no pictures of them. All she knew were their names and as far as she knew, she never told anyone she knew those names. Jules and Margi, as her mother once told her. Was Margi Marguerite? Was Julian her great grandfather? That seemed so insane. So was this damn story. Inside she still hoped that in some way this was a story pitch and that at some moment, Julian would tell her that her father sent him as a joke or that this was his idea for the vampire book. But he never did. The reality she longed for never came.

"My Grandma Claudette only ever told me one detail about her father. He had one piece of jewelry that he always wore that she wished she had been able to find before they died."

Julian reached into his coat pocket and pulled out a small blue pouch. He pulled the tie open and dumped the contents into his open palm. There was an old coin, a tiny loose red gemstone, a postage stamp in a small plastic sleeve, a pendulum made of metal, and a silver ring.

Her eyes immediately focused on the ring.

He held his hand out to her and waited to see which item she would choose, like waiting for the incarnate of the Dali Lamma to pick the right item owned by the previous leader.

She reached out and picked up the ring. It was silver and a large man's ring. The top had a stone set in a unique inverted triangle shape. It was clear and lightly crackled from age. She looked on the inside of the band and read the inscription.

J.L. You inspire my soul to speak. All my love, M.L.

Inhaling deeply Devin breathed out the words, "What do I have to do?"

"Trust me."

"I trust you."

She handed the ring back to him and settled into a comfortable spot on the bed. Now with no pillow to block her from another attack, as she knew there would not be one.

Julian told her about these underground clubs that operate under the nose of the city. The vampires, rarely if ever come out into the public, but the commerçants de sang always meet in these places. They are clocked in the secrecy of darkness and only those involved in the world know of their existence.

"I need to take you to one. To let everyone know who you are, who I am, and that we are in the market to do business. Hopefully, this will lead us to Marguerite."

"When do we leave?" she asked him.

Devin had no idea how much went into being a commerçant de sang.

The lesson would begin. Julian ran through a laundry list of appropriate behaviors and how business dealings were approached. How to look. How to speak. When to speak. How not to die.

She felt as if she was back in school and this semester's lesson was finding the dead. She was nervous, but the intensity of the love that Julian felt for Marguerite was coming off his flesh like electricity. She wrote about love like this everyday, but had never experienced it herself. Maybe he would prove to be even more valuable that she had suspected. Maybe on this vampire novel, but maybe even for future romance gigs at Baxter.

"Before we go, we need to dress you," he said.

She looked down at her clothes and saw small droplets of blood on her thigh.

"Yeh, I should probably change these," she said agreeably as she attempted to wipe the blood off her pants.

"No no, not just that," Julian said. "A makeover. Come with me." He held his hand out and she reached up and took it with hers. "Let's go shopping," he said smiling.

They took the elevator back down into the heart of the sci-fi convention. The stark bright fluorescent lighting and the cold reality of the hotel was almost more than Devin could stand. It was late and there were few attendees wandering the halls in costume. One girl wore a tight black leather outfit and her hair was tinted reddish-purple. As Devin walked past her, she heard someone refer to her as Vamp Willow. Must be from a show or something she thought.

They walked down the long hallway towards the ballrooms that were filled with vendor tables. He stopped at one room called the Cosenza Ballroom and pushed the heavy door open with one hand. The other hand still held onto hers.

Inside the room were about twenty vendors. Most of them sold period clothing and a few sold fake medieval weapons and jewelry. Devin eyed the strange items with a sense of longing. There was such history and fantasy woven into everything in the room. She envied the way in which these fans or crazies or marvels were able to invest themselves in a different world, if even for just a short period of time.

Julian still led her along. Maybe towards something like the fantasy.

He led her over to a table with a heavyset redhead sitting behind it. She had on a green velvet renaissance gown and her red hair was twirled in curls atop her head. Her large breasts pushed out over the top over her corset. Devin could tell that she spent hours getting ready for this day and the smile on her face when she saw Julian, told her that this weekend was probably the most important weekend of the year for her. She was a princess for a few days. Unlike earlier, Devin felt a little sorry for her, instead of just thinking it was silly.

"Wendylynn," Julian said lovingly as her leaned in for a double European kiss kiss. "You look fabulous."

She smiled embarrassed and her cheeks flushed as red as her hair.

"You do have a way with words Jule," she said looking towards the floor. "What can I do for you?" she asked, trying to slip quickly back into business mode, to stave off her reddening cheeks.

"My friend here," he said stepping back and presenting Devin, "is in need of a new outfit."

Wendylynn stood up and walking about the table. She looked Devin up and down quickly.

"Size 8?"

"Yes"

"What kind-of look are you going for?"

"I'm not sure. Maybe gothy?"

Julian leaned in and whispered something in Wendylynn's ear. It seemed to explain everything, as she led Devin towards a row of garment racks with long dark dresses billowing out.

"See anything you like?" she slid her fingertips across the edge of the dresses. The fabric brushed against them, velvet, black, dark blue, blood red (fitting), purple, and dark green.

"I...I'm not sure," she stuttered out, "this is a new look for me."

Devin thumbed through the dresses in a daze. They were all so far out of her normal dress that the decision seemed impossible.

"How about this one dear?" Wendylynn said holding up the floor length brushed velvet blood red gown. It tapered at the waist in a faux corset and had long back ties that wrapped up to the bottom of the breasts. The sleeves were made of a sheer black chiffon that puffed out slightly and cuffed tightly at the wrists.

It was low cut, much lower than Devin ever wore. She blushed and reluctantly took the hanger.

Wendylynn gestured to a mocked up dressing room in the corner of the room. She slowly walked towards it, looking back over her shoulder at Julian for reassurance.

He nodded certainly and knocked a small crooked smile.

Devin slowly slipped into the red dress. It had been a long time since she wore anything but jeans or sweats, let alone a period gown. She stood for a long time in front of the mirror seeing a view of herself that she never saw before.

"Everyday is Halloween," she chuckled under her breath.

"It is," she heard from behind as Julian pushed open the curtain and looked her up and down. He hooked the clasp on the back of the dress with a fluid motion and stepped back to enjoy the view.

She instinctively threw her hands over her chest in cover and her cheeks burned as red as the dress. Her head fell towards the floor. He reached his hand out and lifted her chin.

"You look beautiful," he said.

She felt the flush in her cheeks subside.

"Come," he said extending his other hand out and taking hers. He led her out of the dressing room and back towards the vendor's table.

The look on Wendylynn's face was priceless. She opened her arms and gave Devin a huge bear hug.

"That's the one. That's the one." she exclaimed.

Julian silently slipped a wad of cash into her hand and they walked out of the room with Devin's old clothes in a plastic shopping bag.

They exited the hotel in silence and caught a cab. It was dark outside and Devin did not have on a watch. Had it really been a full day or was it the same night still? Her sense of time was gone and she was tied up in this pitch or reality or dream. If this was a drug, she might just be addicted to it.

They rode in quiet downtown. The bustling city whizzed by as they ignored. They stepped out of the cab onto the curb in front of a large row of warehouses. The buildings were old and slightly revamped…no pun intended. It was dirty. Devin felt herself looking over her shoulder for the monster in the dark, but maybe that monster was the one still holding her hand.

"Where are we?" Devin asked.

"Just down the street from the Ptolemy Club," he answered her, gesturing down the block. "It is an underground club for my kind, commerçants de sang, and those who worship the lifestyle. It is basically a place of business for the commerçants de sang to trade."

This was all so real for Devin, rather surreal. It did feel like Halloween.

"Before we go inside, remember you need to be cold and detached. You understand the basics of the world I live in and must treat the others with respect but never never trust them. Each commerçant de sang has an edge something they or their vampire can do in service of others, but they all are manipulative and dangerous."

"I know all this. You told me. I'm ready. Only, my service my skill, what is mine? You never told me."

"Isn't it obvious? You are a journalist Dev," he said. "You can use your contacts at the various newspapers to provide cover stories for crimes that my kind may have committed. The perfect mis-direction they need. You can spoil the pot, so to speak and create that doubt. It will keep their deadly deeds secret to the watching eyes of the human world."

Journalist, she thought. Not anymore. A ghostwriter, a fake, helping all these other writers lie to the world. She had become everything she hated in writers. Liars. Fakes.

"Don't talk tonight. Just observe. Don't talk unless I give the nod. And," Julian paused for a second reaching into his coat pocket. He pulled out a small silver pendant hanging on a short chain. "You must wear this at all times."

He twisted her around and slipped the chain around her bare neck. It was cold, like his skin.

"Always keep this showing. It is what shows that you are a commerçant de sang and will keep any of my kind from killing you outright and will make the commerçants de sang talk to you."

Devin reached up and felt the pendant with her fingertips. It was sharp and pointed like a V on the bottom. Sharp like thorns on a rose. One side looped into an oval and the other side stretched out into a curved line. She wondered if it was a Chinese character, but was too embarrassed to ask.

"Do you understand? Are you ready?"

She nodded silently.

"Remember everything I told you."

Devin wondered inside her head why exactly they were there. Maybe so she could see this real world Julian had opened up for her. Maybe to trade for something that would make her sick and wish she never accepted Baxter's offer to write this vampire novel. Maybe...maybe Marguerite.

"Good," he said and gestured down the dark empty block.

They walked past a few buildings until the subtle soft sound of gothic music pulsed from behind a closed doorway. The building looked like an old hotel. A five-step walkup made of concrete and old dark wood. It seemed to blend into the facade of the neighborhood like it was veiled by magick. Maybe it was.

Julian placed his palm on the tinted glass 12"x12" window at the top of the door. The door creaked open and the face of a angry looking man with short spiky black hair and sunglasses nodded and stepped aside to allow them in. The door slammed behind hard and there was no turning back.

It was an old hotel, Devin could now see. The heavy woodwork curled towards the ceiling, which was made of old patterned tin. The flowers in the lobby were covered in dust and cobwebs, as if on purpose to create ambiance. It was everything dark and terrifying that Devin longed to know, yet longed to run from. They walked down a short hall towards the sound of pulsing music. This was a far cry from the reasonably clean mid-level hotel they had recently left. Devin longed for the safety of that hotel just then.

"Now we'll sit, have a few drinks, and then you can get down to business," Julian said.

"Business? Now, are you kidding?" she said sharply but whispering.

Her heart thumped in her chest louder than the music escaping its way from the speakers overhead.

"You are ready."

"I am not!"

"Yes you are. Trust me."

"You told me to observe. Just watch. You're a liar. What the hell kind of business are we here for Julian? You should have warned me."

He grabbed her wrist and pulled her in close. She had assumed that there would be some time for her to absorb the environment and the people.

"You said you're ready. Besides, I changed my mind. Don't worry, I have told you enough for this. We need to find leads, to see if anyone knows where Marguerite is."

Yes, Devin thought...to find her.

The air in the club felt very thick and heavy, like there was a purposeful lack of oxygen. She inhaled as deeply as she could as they slipped onto barstools at a small round table in the center of the room. Several similar round wooden tables circled around them where other couples sat engrossed in their drinks and conversations.

A long oak bar ran the entire length of the room. Stragglers hung off its edge leaning over half empty glasses of dark liquid. Their eyes poisoned and lidded. In the far end of the room a few partygoers swayed to some dark ambient gothic rhythms that were being strung by a DJ shrouded in a small glass booth draped with black velvet curtains. The walls were sponge painted blood red and black and old carved wood outlined the walls and peaked around the vintage tin ceiling. It sparkled slightly off the dancing lights that popped out to the beat of the music.

"This place is so weird," Devin whispered. "Everyone looks so Bram Stoker's *Dracula*." She breathed out a light chuckle. A constant stream of cold air swirled around her. It was that same feeling she got when she and Julian were alone. It told her a vampire was near. Now several were near and she was terrified and exhilarated at the same time. Plus, this is great material for her book. All she had to do was change all the names to *Buffy* characters and maybe she could pull it off. Then, Baxter would let her publish one of her own novels. Finally. Some real recognition and not just the invisible name hidden in the words.

She giggled again nervously.

"No jokes," Julian snapped with a discerning look.

"Can I get you two some drinks?"

A voice appeared from nowhere and to the right. A tall slender woman with a round tray balancing on three fingers stared down at Devin, like she was a dog. Her eyes were sea blue and looked like her tears were swimming around in them. You could get lost in the swirling. She must be a vampire too. She wore short shorts and a tight black corseted top. She was gorgeous, much more attractive that Devin. Julian's eyes immediately went to her.

Devin fidgeted in her own corset. It was tightening with her struggling breath. She had never worn something so provocative before. She wasn't sure she could keep up the self-confidence that comes with such a look.

Julian, feeling sustained in his approval of the waitress, simply nodded at her and with an unspoken understanding, she walked away. She returned what seemed like seconds later with a tall thin glass of dark liquid for Julian and a small wine glass for Devin.

"Is this?" she started to ask.

"No, it's red wine."

"And yours?"

"Drink," he said as he slipped the waitress cash in a subtle fluid motion. She smiled and disappeared into the crowd.

Devin lifted the glass to her lips and smelled it. Wine, she thought. Thank God! She took a small sip and nervously placed the glass back down on the table with both hands. She fidgeted around the stem, waiting for something to happen.

"Long time no see my sexy one," a familiar voice echoed from behind Devin.

Before she could even raise her head, the figure of Marisol slid onto Julian's lap. Her fingers grabbed his hair and she lightly nibbled on his right ear. You could smell the want on her.

"I knew you could not stay away my dear," she whispered into it.

"Off Marisol."

"Come on my lover. You know you want me on top of you," she yanked his head back with her fingers still wrapped through his hair. Her tongue slowly made its way towards his neck.

He yanked her hand from his hair and moved out of the way of her tongue.

"I said off now!"

Reluctantly, she hopped back down to the hard wood floor. Still the smell of moth baths surrounded her. Devin thought that there much be more to their relationship than Julian was saying.

It seemed like Marisol loved Julian, but hated him at the same time. Some angry truth hid just below each of their eyelids. Maybe someday he would tell her the whole story.

"I thought you were hunting at the convention?" he asked her.

"I tired. No one held my interest enough," Marisol said with a pouting lip. She twirled a long curl between her fingers and stared at Devin with hunger.

Devin knew that Julian certainly held her interest, but she needed to feed. She probably killed someone at that convention. Lured them into a dark hotel room with the promise of sex. Sunk her long sharp teeth into their neck, just as Julian had done to her. Instead of just showing her dark face, she consumed them and left them for dead in the still darkened room. The body falling limply to the hard floor. Blood spilling onto the cheap carpeting. A present left for housekeeping to find.

But, part of Devin wanted to feel it again too. Julian's fangs in her neck, anyone's fangs in her neck. That slowing of her heart beat. The warmth that came just before the pain. The haze in vision and exhilaration when the pain finally came. Then the pleasure, just past it.

Marisol wrapped her arms around Julian. She wanted him with that same fire.

"Marisol go away," he said.

"I thought I would cash in a few owes, plus I love to dance. You used to love to dance. Come Julian, dance with me," she tried to pull him off his stool, but he sat steadfast.

"No."

"You're no fun," she huffed. "Well, you know where to find me." And with a quick breeze, she stepped backwards and vanished back into the crowd.

Devin's heart raced at the reality of all this. She was still a little numb from the blood drinking at the hotel that proved Julian's story to her. But this was even more real. This was all like a dream. The bite marks pulsed on her throat like a heartbeat. Like she was living the book she was writing. Like she was being *Buffy* and that whole world was real. Is real. Is it? Will she wake up back at home in her bed and this was all a dream? Maybe she fell asleep while working on that latest crappy romance novel and Baxter never really called her. Maybe she was in a coma having a vivid long dream. A tiny panic attack rippled up from her stomach and kissed her lips. She touched them with her fingertips. They were wet and felt real.

"There are only a few of my kind here," he told her. "There are several commerçants de sang." He nodded his head towards the back of the room.

She turned her head and saw a small women and a tall thin man disappear behind a heavy black curtain. Soon Devin assumed, they would do business.

"So the rest are…human?"

"Yes."

"Why are they here?"

"Some are here because they desperately want to be a part of this world and others do not yet know why they have been brought here"

"For…for food?"

He simply stared back at her for what seemed like minutes. She knew that most of the people in this old hotel bar would be dead by morning and there was not a damn thing she could do about it.

"I know all this is hard for you to understand and accept. I am not saying any of it is right, but it is what it is. All I want to do is to find my wife and get us both out of this world," he waved his hand through the air.

She saw trails from his fingertips.

"What about the rest of them," Devin asked him.

"I can only worry about her" Julian answered, "Only her. The rest must be left for those who follow me."

Marisol spun in from behind and wrapped her arms around Julian's neck. His expression went to pissed off in one sharp second.

"Ready for that dance now lover? Or how about a lap dance. I remember how you like that," she teased.

Before Devin could hear his response, she felt a tug on her right shoulder that nearly flipped her off the barstool. Her head was jerked around fast and her eyes locked on a set of dark black eyes in front of the face of a pale man with long flowing blond hair. She saw his long fangs drip from his lips and she was frozen in time.

Devin felt faint and was flung suddenly forward and landed with her head on the round table. The room was spinning. She felt lost in that fog that she felt back in the hotel room when Julian drank from her throat. She reached up and felt her neck. It was warm again. As her hand came back down and her eyes focused, she saw a small amount of blood spill through her fingertips onto the cold sticky tabletop. She looked towards where Julian was sitting and he was gone. She inhaled nervously, sucking in that heavy air and turned slowly around.

She saw Julian's long black coat flying behind him as he tackled the blond haired man. He hissed from behind his hidden face. Julian's fist came down hard against the blond man's face. His head rocked hard to the right and a CSI-style blood spatter hit the wood grain wallboard.

Half the dancers on the floor stopped cold, heads up, and sniffed the air. After a few seconds they realized it was not a buffet and went back to bobbing to the dark ambient music spun by the DJ. He was a tall slender man that stood above a keyboard in the glass coffin on the stage. His dyed blond hair spilled over his eyes. The word *Molarmill* was etched on a crudely made sign beside him. He was so pale. He was probably a vampire too. They all seemed mesmerized by his rhythms. It jumbled in Devin's head. It reminded her of many drunken high school nights long ago.

Devin still spun and the last thing she remembered before passing out was Marisol leaning in placing a cocktail napkin over her new wound.

"My dear, you won't last long in our world," she said and faded out to nothingness.

Not knowing how long she was out this time, Devin peeled open her dry eyes and found herself in Julian's lap. He held a tearing of a white shirt to her wound soaking up the blood the vampire stranger had stolen. He held her like a child, but also like a lover.

"Where, what is, where is…she?" she asked.

"Gone. I am so sorry. I should not have allowed that to happen. I am so sorry Dev," he paused, "However, we now have done business."

"What?"

Not remembering going into that curtained room. So much of this night was a fog, so much of the past few days.

Then, a short brown haired boy appeared at their side.

"I am sorry sir," he said. "My boss did not realize who you were," he said to Julian, "and that you were spoken for," he nodded apologetically to Devin. "We are in your debt," he looked to the right and set his eyes on the blond haired man who sat hunched over on a small velvet loveseat. His face was badly bruised and bloodied.

"What happ…?" Devin stuttered.

"All we seek in information," Julian told him. "I am looking for one called Marguerite. She is one of the elders."

"As I know you are sir. I have heard of her," he said. "She is one of the last original ones."

"Yes." Julian said.

"I, nor my boss have ever seen her, but I know that those who follow her used to live in the penthouse of a high rise on State Street. Just past where the old Cook Theater used to be. That is all I know. I swear it sir."

"Then we are even," Julian said with a harsh tone in his voice. "For now."

The boy nodded, turned and walked towards the blond haired man. He gave a nervous look back towards Julian, just in case he decided to exact revenge.

"That was doing business?" She asked Julian.

"No and yes. Normally it is simple negotiating and trading in the backroom. Service for service. I am sorry that it had to go this way. It is my fault and I hope you can forgive me."

She let the concept of forgiveness run through her head for a few seconds.

"I can. I forgive you."

She couldn't even believe that she could, but she did.

"Come," Julian said and helped Devin rise to her feet. Her head was spinning. He slipped his arm around her waist and led her towards the door. He held her up almost completely. She felt her feet gliding along the floor like she was floating.

She rolled in and out of consciousness. Her eyelids felt so incredibly heavy.

She vaguely remembered the train ride home and awoke in the morning alone on her bed, still wearing the blood red dress.

Chapter Eight

The alarm did not go off. Its sterile angry yell did not break the silence of Devin's dreaming. A sluggish feeling like a hangover woke her instead. She slowly sat up in her bed, brushing the wrinkles out of the velvet dress she still wore. Her face felt flushed and her vision was a little bit blurry.

So much of last night seemed like a crazy dream. She did not trust her own memory.

"Good morning...ugh," she said to no one in particular. Partly to herself, but with a small part of her hoping she would hear Julian's voice appear from nowhere and he would save her from the darkness she was swirling in. She always thought he would save her.

Speckles of her night's dream still hung in her memory. Julian was there, as he always was somehow. She was hunting, hunting vampires. All the fear and rage that hung inside of her was exploding in her fight. She found one, a vampire outside the Ptolemy Club. She grabbed a dagger that was strapped to her inner thigh and plunged it into his chest. In his state of confusion and pain, she sliced his throat in a quick moment. Then, he hit her hard. She lost balance and fell back onto the cold grey cement. He was on her, but before he could make that final strike, Julian appeared like a monster of the darkness. He grabbed the vampire and removed his head with one last strike. He saved her again. A hunter she could not be without him as her safety net. Even in her dreams.

She stood up slowly feeling her bones creak and walked towards the unflattering full-length mirror that taunted her most days. She looked dead. Pale and tired. She pulled her hair off her shoulder and stared at two sets of bite marks. They were healing quickly. She pulled her hair back into her typical ponytail. She tried to see the Devin she used to see everyday, but she was not there anymore. Someone else had taken her place. She had no idea who this new someone was yet.

She slipped quietly out of the dress and tossed it atop the pile of clothes that always remained on the bedroom floor. Normal clothes for the normal world.

The clock showed that the time was 8 a.m. almost exactly. She shrugged and she slipped into a simple shirt and simple shorts. She lifted the dead limp curls out of her eyes.

She walked out to her living room and looked for Julian. He was not there. Where did he go? When did he bring her home? How did he know where she lived? The blinds were open, so he couldn't be here. Too much direct sunlight would kill him. She knew a few minutes of sunlight was ok, but he told here that more than that will cause severe deadly burns. He couldn't? No.

The phone shocked her out of her search for him and she stumbled over to her wooden desk. She flopped down into the hard chair, like she did every night when writing. It shocked her spine as usual. The pain today was especially strong.

"Hello?" she said into the phone.

"Devy, baby."

Ugh! Baxter, The last person she wanted to hear from right now. The bright reality of him was more than she could take. Trying to sort out the details of book writing was something she couldn't handle.

"What do you need Baxter?"

"How is the vamp book going babe? You getting' your research on? Lay it out for me sweetness," she hated when he tried to be cool, to be street.

"Fine. I am learning a lot about…vampire lore."

She caught herself. She almost gave away more than he knew. Or maybe he did know. Maybe Baxter knew all along about Julian, about her great grandparents, about them.

"Look Bax, I just got up and am really busy. This is a bad time. Let me ring you later, ok?"

Before he had a chance to respond, she clicked the end button on the phone. No Baxter right now. He was too real too everyday life. She was not quite back there yet. She still hung on to a small piece of last night and that crazy dream. She didn't know what was more crazy, what really happened or the dream.

She reached into the desk drawer and took out a few spare sheets of paper. She needed to document what happened, just in case. She scribbled as fast as she could. The images and words flowing much faster than they normally did when she was working on one of her romance novels. Reality was easier to write about. After feeling satisfied that she got enough down on paper, she hid the pages back in the drawer, where no one could find them. She felt as if she carried a heavy burden of truth in this secret Julian had given her.

She stood up and felt the creak in her back. She took a comfortable position on the couch and waited. The clock ticked slowly with each second. It rang in her ears with a deafening silence like her own beating heart. She felt as if she was a stone statue in waiting. The sun eventually and slowly peaked under the tall buildings and night greeted her with a warmth she accepted thankfully. She had no idea how many hours she had sat there. She hadn't eaten and hadn't wanted to. She had a new hunger now and waited for it to be satisfied.

She heard the front door creak slowly open just as the sun disappeared completely. Without looking, she knew it was Julian. That cool breeze blew in from nowhere. He made his way over to the window and looked out on the city.

"How did I get home last night?" she asked him.

Julian turned around, ignoring her question and strutted over and sat on the edge of the couch facing Devin.

"So, tonight we go back to the club for more information. We are on the right track and if we act quickly and smartly, we may get what we need, " he said matter of factly.

"Are you freaking kidding me?" she spurts out. "I'm not going back there. Not after what happened. I'm not crazy or suicidal."

She stands up and goes to turn and walk away, but Julian grabs her wrist and twists her back around and down onto the couch next to him. She could not spin from his grasp, like she could from Marisol's. Or maybe she did not really want to. The bite marks on her neck pulsed with a left over pain.

"Last night was a fluke. I will never let anyone hurt you again," he reassures Devin. "I cannot afford to lose you now. We are closer than I have been in sixty years. This is the time now."

His voice begins to sound determined. Also underneath, desperate, but angry.

She knew that without her he was trapped in a state of limbo. The vampires would not talk to him, neither would the traders. He essentially was mute to the world he needed to enter. An outcast, like she felt like most days.

"You have to understand Devin, I have been searching for a family member, because that is the only way I can barter myself close enough to Marguerite. I need you."

"Why didn't you just tell me that from the start," she asks him. "Why the lies?"

"I had no choice. You never would have believed me. I had to make all the right arrangements in order to get to you and get to the truth."

"Did you arrange for Dena and the other writer to get sick?"

"It was necessary for me to get close enough to you."

"Why? For what? How could you?"

"There are only a handful of us originals left. The rest of the vampires are our offspring from those first hungry weeks. They cannot make more of us. If I get Marguerite back, that helps everyone. Two less originals to curse anyone."

"I wish I could just believe that," Devin contracts back to him. "But what about those Nazis? They can just keep making more. You act like if we find your wife, it all goes away. That's not true. If you really want to make a difference, what about them?"

"The Nazis were the strongest of all of us. Now, that Maks and François are out of the community, they need her. They also need more science, more modern science. They want to find a way to make more like them. To grow their population. Marguerite is the link to that. If we severe it, maybe it will help."

"Won't they just eventually die?"

"Someday, they will die too. I just need to keep them from getting any assistance, until that day. They may die at my hands. I don't know. They may die hundreds of years from now. We can't predict our lifespan, not anymore."

"Well, has Marguerite been on the same page with them?" Devin asks him.

"Yes," he responds but hesitates, "But I know her. I know that if we are together again, she will see things more clearly. They have her brainwashed. I am certain of it."

"And how are you different then Julian?" she said accusatorily. "You have killed people. You haven't told me anything in detail, but I can see it in your face. They are things you are not telling me about Marisol, things about your past. Why shouldn't I be just as worried about you?"

"You should not worry."

"Maybe I should," Devin says, standing up from the couch and crossing her arms in front of her.

"Maybe."

"Maybe I'll just take care of it myself."

Julian chuckled.

Her voice seethed with confidence. She can do this, she thought. She was tougher than he thought. She had reluctantly become somewhat of a novice vampire hunter. A reluctant blood trader. She certainly could do more.

Julian stands up and gets right in her face.

"You're kidding yourself Devin."

He smiles and stands his ground. This cocky look spread wildly over his face. It irritated the hell out of Devin.

"Don't tell me what I can and cannot do. Remember, you came to find me. You needed me. I was the only one that could get you back into the vampire fold."

"You have no idea what these people are and what they are after. And while I need you because you are my blood, you could not last five minutes in the club or anywhere else without my help. Without me."

"Ppff," Devin spurts, knowing he is wrong. Right?

He reached out and grabbed her shoulder, spinning her around to face him.

"You want that realism for you book? That all seems pretty trivial now doesn't it?" he asked her. "You have material now don't you? Don't start confusing the information I have shared with you with any ability to fight this war."

"Whose war Julian? Is it for you or for mankind?"

"All I need is for you to work with the blood traders. Find her. Help get me access and then you are done. I will give you the facts I have on vampire lore, so you can knock out the details on that stupid book for Baxter and I will give you this," he said.

He reached into his inside breast pocket and pulled out a small journal. It was tan leather and slightly curled from age and having been cramming into a pocket for so many years. The paper was aged yellow. It looked like the same book he tossed on the table that night in the hotel room.

"What's that?" Devin asked him her eyes never having left the view of the book.

"It's my journal," Julian responded. "My journal for the last 15 years. Everything I have seen, everything I have done and been is in here."

He flipped the three hundred or so pages with his thumb. They were filled solid with words. His face had a longing as he skimmed the pages.

Devin longed to see them too. Find out what they told. She sensed that hundreds of great new books lie within those tattered pages. What she could do with that. She struggled to keep herself from reaching out and grabbing the book from his hands.

"What do you mean give it to me?" she asked him softly.

"You will have enough everything you need to write this vampire book and a hundred ones after that," he said.

She knew Marisol was in there and so many more horrible stories that she longed to know. The dark side of the city that she hungered for and was terrified of at the same time. Just like the power of the lust and passion in the romance novels she wrote, but never felt in the flesh. It was intoxicating. She wanted to drink all night.

"You are my blood, the last of my bloodline, my family, and when I go, all I have is yours."

He slid the book back into his pocket and looked into her eyes with a parental compassion.

Devin exhaled deeply, realizing that there was no way for her to get her hands on that journal right now. She must wait.

"You are my blood," she said back to him.

Another very cold realization swept over her. She understood now that he never meant for him and Marguerite to go off and live happily ever after in some cute little cottage in France. She had been so wrong in her belief.

He meant to die once he found her, for them both to die. To end a long long life of darkness as one. In return he was willing to give Devin his entire life as payment for damning her and her family. Even justice.

Devin looked towards the floor. The room hung in silence. She heard the door quietly slide closed as Julian left.

"Good-bye," she whispered.

He always left without saying good-bye. But he always came back.

Eventually. But, several days passed and Julian did not come around.

Each day, Devin paced the hard wood floors of her apartment in silence, unable to think about anything but him. Unable to write. Unable to take Baxter's irritating progress phone calls at all hours of the day and night. The stark facade of the old real life seemed so empty.

Finally, she rattled off the last fifty pages of the romance novel that she had been finishing when Baxter gave her this new assignment in a matter of hours. The words flooded from her mind like water, shallow and unimportant. But even still, she knew the words were good enough and Baxter would be more than satisfied. She barely cared anymore about her job.

"My dearest, I pledge to never again leave you. You are the sun that rises, the leaves that fall their gentle way to the ground, the perseverance of the rain that breaks its way through the protection of the clouds."

"Darling, you have returned to me. The old gardener told me you were dead. How I am filled with joy at your presence."

His large swollen arms embraced her. The sweat dripped off him. His hair was wet with it. He reached down as lifted her chin upwards. His skin glowed peach and sunshine and wonderful.

"With love always", he said.

She shuddered inside his arms. Her safe place of protection. How long she had waited for his return. How many times she feared that it would never happened. Her prayers had been answered. Her faith restored.

The rebels had long since been gone and for the first time in years, she felt utter safety.

The sun pitched forward in the sky. It haloed over the small shack he had built and where they will share their lives. This day forth, love is all that matters. Bright futures all around.

Bigger things bigger stories lie ahead, if *he* would only return to her.

She had yet to even pen a word of this new vampire novel, but stories flooded her head. She wanted so desperately to write about the real world that she was seeing, but knew it could only damage Julian. She knew no matter what he did, she could never intentionally hurt him. They were blood after all and blood always remains. Always returns.

Chapter Nine

After several days, Devin found herself staring out the floor to ceiling windows one night near midnight when she heard the familiar sound of the front door slide slowly open. She knew he did not have a key, but somehow he managed to gain stealthy entry each and every time.

"Where have you been?" she asked Julian with the tone and dictation of a parent's discern tone.

"Taking care of things."

"What things?"

"Here," he tossed a dry cleaning bag onto the coffee table. The hanger banged against the glass and rattled for a minute.

Devin turned and looked down at the garment. It was the blood red velvet dress she wore that first night to the club. Her blood had been washed clean and the smell of smoke and death gone. How in the world did he get it? She left it in the bedroom, hidden beneath all the clothes from her real life.

Had he been here? Watching me sleep.

"Get dressed," he said. "We are going out."

He disappeared into the kitchen and waited.

Devin picked the dress up off the table and walked into her bedroom. Her stocking feet shuffled against the floor. A familiar sound. She unwrapped the plastic from the makeshift bag and ran her fingers down the dress. It felt starched and fresh, but she knew it wasn't. She could see in her head where the dress had been, like it had its own life and identity. When she wore it, she became someone else. Maybe something else. The vampire hunter. The spy. The avenger. The blood trader.

She slipped off her clothes and tossed them into the familiar pile on the floor. She turned to see if Julian was watching her. He was nowhere. She crinkled the velvet fabric between her hands. She slid into it in one movement and suddenly felt Julian's cold hand on her back.

He hooked the clasp and then disappeared faster than he had appeared. How was it that he was always there just when needed?

She looked down towards the bed and saw something that surprised her. A dagger. It was about twelve inches long and had an ornate handle. It was resting on top of a strap that Devin believed was meant to strap to her thigh. It was just like the dagger in her dreams. She ran her finger down the blade. It was sharp. Just as sharp as the lucid one that slit the throats of many a vampire at night. She slid it on her thigh in silence. The blade was cold, but it made her feel safer.

She smoothed the dress down and pulled her hair up off her shoulders and into a loose twist on top of her head. The small bite marks were fading but still visible. She touched them and they stung a little bit. Her badge of honor. She stood there, staring at her reflection. Despite the pageantry of the dress, it did make her feel beautiful. Much better than the typical jeans and t-shirt combo that she wore everyday she actually got dressed. More regal.

Julian walked back into the bedroom and came up behind her. He reached around her and slid the silver pendant across her throat. The cold metal made her shiver or maybe it was the coldness of his fingertips. Rough, icy, yet inviting.

She let him hook the clasp and took his hand in silence, walking out the front door. She didn't bother taking her keys. She didn't thank him for the dagger. She knew one day she may need to use it against him. He probably knew that as well.

It was eerily quiet, just like that night she first met Julian in Baxter's office. Her shoes clacked against the sidewalk.

They hit the transit stop in no time. They arrived downtown on the quick 10 and walked the few blocks to the old hotel.

People walked the street, just as any other night, but they seemed oblivious to the horror that sat just beyond the hotel door. If they only knew what Devin now knew, they would not walk so carelessly alone or with no worries. They would realize that monsters do exist to chase you in the darkness. That no matter what, they will always come. They know the darkness better that you.

Julian placed his hand on the darkened glass window on the club door and the same dark haired man opened the door and invited them inside with a nod. Instead of finding a seat at one of the round tables, Julian led her to the back where the heavy curtains hid the blood traders secret meetings. The DJ pulsed ambient dark swirls of music from the speakers. Swirls of dancers cluttered the floor, swaying to the heavy beat. The air felt thick like the other night.

Devin had become used to the heat and the smell. Stale mothballs and death.

As Julian pushed open the heavy curtain they were greeted by the face of the young boy that they met the other night. The one that apologized for his vampire master attacking Devin.

Devin shuddered for a second and thought it was a trap.

No never. He wouldn't.

The young boy nodded a hello.

She stepped inside. When she turned around looking for Julian, he was gone. It appeared to be a backroom converted sloppily into a meeting room. A large round poker table sat in the far corner with metal folding chairs circled around it. Unrecognizable stains scattered their way across the green felt top. The walls were splattered with promotional posters for every large scale event recently held in the city.

Two people already sat at the table and looked at her, waiting for her to take a seat.

One was a woman who looked as if time aged her more that the calendar. She had short red hair and looked of Irish decent. She wore a simple black shirt and pants. She chugged a large glass of bronze liquid and slammed it hard on the tabletop.

The other table sitter was a heavyset man who reminded Devin of Jake Baxter. His hair was salt and pepper, but too much so for his age, which Devin guessed was about 35. His hands were fat and chapped and he wore a poorly cut suit in a dark blue.

They both stared her up and down in judgment. They recognized the newbie in their midst.

Devin forced up the confidence she held just beyond her grasp. She grew stronger each day with him. She held a strong face. The handle of the dagger pressed into her outer thigh. She used that slight pain, like a rock in your shoe in a lie detector test. A little pain, was always good to use.

The young boy gestured for her to take a seat at the table.

She walked over, nervous inside, and began to hone her acting calm and confidence skills. She slid out the metal chair. It screeched loudly against the concrete flooring. She took a seat.

"Looks like it's just us tonight," the red haired woman said.

She smashed a cigarette hard into a glass ashtray. The smoke drizzled upwards towards the ceiling.

Devin noticed that she wore the same silver pendant that she did. The symbol of commerçants de sang. A brand. A mark.

"Let's get to it. Ron," she said, looking at the salt and pepper man, "did you get those pictures I asked for?"

Ron reached under the table and pulled out a manila folder. He tossed it towards the red haired girl, making it only half way across the large table.

She pulled it the remaining distance and casually flipped it open. Inside were several daytime photos of a woman in her mid-40's kissing a much younger man. They seemed to have been taken at an angle hidden somewhere behind a large object. Spying.

"Good," red said and closed the folder, placing it inside an old black leather briefcase bag to her left.

"That makes our current owes even Leeana. Clean slate,"

"What about you?" Leeana asked turning and facing Devin. "What do you have to bargain with tonight?"

"Well," she thought of a million ways to say things that would make her sound accomplished and strong, but all she could mutter out was, "I...I'm a writer, ugh the papers, cool stories."

"Greeeat" Leeana said.

Deep breath Devin.

"I am a journalist I mean. I have been around. I can utilize my contacts in the newspaper biz to modify...ugh stories...for you," Devin slurred out and smiled.

"You mean like cover stories?" Ron inquired, leaning into the table. His fat roll squishing up against the wooden railing.

"Yes," she answered him.

"Ok, I can use that," he said. "My boss has a habit of leaving a bit of a mess behind, so to speak. Mostly homeless but maybe just something to take the eyes off."

"Good," Devin sank in that confidence. She knew she could do this. Her very first trade. Not bad.

"I'll trade for two of those. For now."

Devin went over in her head the so-called rules that Julian told her about. The blood traders. Ron telling her that he'll trade for two means we wants two units of her service. That means he owes her two of whatever he does. She can collect now or later. How was she supposed to remember all of this?

"That works. So, what is your trade?" she asked him.

"I have several," he responded.

He reached into his coat pocket and pulled out a small spiral book. He flipped it open and took out a small chewed on pencil.

"We can handle large financial transfers through various small corporations. The turnaround time is fairly fast, based on the amount."

Money laundering Devin surmised.

He gestured the notebook towards her. She did not take the time to try and read it, but just nodded in acceptance.

"We can also facilitate nighttime boat usage on the lake for, ugh trips. We have several small vessels that are legally leased and virtually impossible to identify specifically."

Body dumping.

"Also, daytime long-term surveillance services."

Spying.

"Ugh, I guess the second one," she said.

He scribbled the details down in his small notebook. Devin thought that Julian should have told her about that little detail. She would need to remember what people owed her or more importantly, what she owed them.

Julian leaned casually against the long oak bar. A pretty girl with soft brown curls in his eyesight. It only took a few minutes for her to respond to his unspoken call. Slowly she strolled over making sure her walk was seductive and mysterious or at least as seductive as a human could be. She joined him at the bar.

"I'm Anne."

Without responding out loud, she took his hand and led him to a dark corner of the dance floor. He slowly moved her up against the wall and released his nighttime face.

She did not seem surprised.

He sunk his long white fangs deep into her throat and held her wrists against the wall hard. He hated when they struggled.

Leanna leans in towards the table and waves an open hand at Devin.

"I could maybe use a story. Three," she says in a very matter of fact business way. He voice seemed so casual and cold.

"Good," Devin accepted.

She waited for Leanna to tell her what she had to offer. The *thump thump* of the ambient music just outside the curtains kept time with the heavy beat of her heart. Her pulse must be racing. The time seemed to tick minutes away. Then she spoke.

"I can offer you special investigative services. I have a great many contacts in government office and private security. We can find anyone anywhere at anytime."

He knew. Julian must have known.

"I accept," Devin said. "In fact, I may have a use for one…trade…right now."

Ron stood up, seeing his unspoken signal to leave. The chair beneath him skidded across the cement floor.

She paused for a moment, until she was sure that they were alone.

"I…my boss is looking for one of the originals. He is one too."

Leeana's eyebrows raised and she looked intrigued. She must not have had an interesting trade in a while.

Devin coughed, her throat somehow becoming so dry all of a sudden. She wished she had forced Julian to stop at the bar first. That mysterious wine would taste perfect right now.

"Her name, the other one, her ugh name. Marguerite."

"I figured." Leanna said softly. "She is one of the few female originals left. And your boss I assume, is the famous lost and lonely Julian LaShrou."

Leanna's mouth twisted up in an amused smile. It was unclear whether she respected Julian or thought the idea of him was a joke.

"Yes, he is," Devin said. "He is looking to locate Marguerite. Do you have any idea where she is? Is she alive or around, well still?"

"She is in the city. For the little we see of her. She has always been a recluse. That I am sure you know. As is Julian."

Leanna taunted somehow knowing that this was the first time Devin ever traded. Her virginity in this world must have been written all over her not pale enough face. Goth dress-up. She struggled inside to hold a stoic face for the dealings. Just long enough. Just the tip of the blade.

"The 1600 building. Downtown, north of the water tower. There are a few floors of suites that friends share."

She stressed the word friends, implying some sort of vampire hangout or weird undead fraternity. Kappa Gamma Bite-a. No, that would be stupid. Actually, that would make a great young adult vampire novel. Stop it! Get back on track idiot. Focus.

"And Marguerite, she lives there?" Devin asked.

"She is there. They keep her there. At least, last time I heard anything. I can look into for you if you want."

"Who keeps her…"

The curtain flashed open. She turned to see Julian peering through the folds of fabric. Part of her was thankful he was back to protect her and part irritated that he interrupted.

"Julian, what?"

He had a slightly urgent look on his face.

"We are done then," Leanna said and turned to the side, clicking on her cell phone and facing away from the two.

Devin nodded and got up and walked out under Julian's arm raising the dark fabric.

He took her hand and led her towards the front of the club. He pulled hard and with one yank harder could rip Devin's arm right out of the socket.

"Julian," she pulled back. "Stop."

He stopped, looking irritated and turned back at her.

"What?" he asked in a rough tone.

"The 1600 building. Downtown, north of the water tower. That is where Marguerite is supposed to be. But something is wrong. Leanna made it seem like they were holding her there, like a prisoner. I need to get more information."

"We will talk more later," Julian said and returned to pulling her wrist. "We have to go now."

He stressed the word *now* a bit too much.

As they exited the front door, Devin saw Marisol a few feet away in the corner. She wore an evil and knowing grin. It bothered Devin. She knew something had happened between the two of them, while she was in the back room. Maybe a fight about old times. They must have been lovers, she thought. There is no other explanation for the strange vibe that ran between them. It was thicker than the air and hot. Heavy.

The cool air outside hit Devin in the face hard. The air was breathable and lighter than inside the club. She soaked it in for a moment, while Julian continued dragging her down the street towards the place where the cab had dropped them off that first night. Something about the air was too cold, like that breeze that she felt each time a vampire came up behind her. She felt it that first night in Baxter's office when Julian appeared out of the shadows like a dream or a nightmare.

There it was again, she thought. She tugged back on Julian's arm. Pulling herself to a stop.

"Stop, do you feel that?" she asked him.

He turned back to face her, ready to say something with an angry urgency, when his face flushed white and his eyes shot up. His face contorted in slow motion and his fangs dropped from his lips. He hissed. Spit flew out from between his teeth.

Devin whipped her head around just in time to see Marisol's face snicker from behind the fist of a large man. It knocked her hard on the face. She felt a stream of blood run down into her eye. That heavy feeling came over her again. As her head hit the hard grey concrete, she saw Marisol's dress breeze past her face.

"I told you Julian, you need to respect the power that I have at my fingertips," she snapped her fingers.

Devin heard Julian grunting in pain and heard the loud sound of a hard object rocket down on Julian. Fists pummeled him over and over again and Devin could not lift her head off the ground to help him. Then, he became suddenly silent. She heard someone say the name Anne.

Oh God.

For the first time Devin felt this overwhelming fear. Vampire hunter my ass, she thought. She needed to bump up those lessons. Mostly, bump up her fighting skills. It had been years since she did martial arts with her brother. Too many years. She almost forgot how to sense her attacker. Obviously.

Thump thump. Not music this time.

The large man's boots shuffled to the sound of dragging a heavy object a few feet away.

"Julian," Devin moaned out softly.

Then, Marisol bent down and looked her in her blood filled eyes, sideways.

"Hello my dear," she said. "There is someone you simply must meet."

She smiled and as her arms reached out to lift Devin off the ground, the tunnel closed and she slipped into nothingness.

Chapter Ten

Devin rubbed her eyes, feeling the dried blood on her cheek. She squinted the one small oil lamp of light into focus and raised her head up straight.

She was seated in an old wooden chair, similar to the one behind her desk at home. The familiar pain in her back that came from many long nights sitting up typing at the computer, told her that she had been in that chair for hours.

But where was she?

There were no windows in the room. The color of the walls was dark, maybe blood red (blood it figures) and there was an odd stone pattern that climbed up one wall. Large stones and what looked like broken liquor bottles, mixed with pieces of old stained glass. It smelled of an old person's home. Mothballs, like Marisol and something minty, and old lives covered with dust.

Apart from the chair she sat in, the only furniture was a small velvet bench on the opposite side of the small room. A young attractive man sat calmly on it, reading in the near darkness what appeared to be a trade paperback book. After a few minutes he looked up at Devin.

"You're good," he said and tossed the book at her feet.

It landed cover up and she could see that it was *Riding Horses to the Train Station*. It was the third novel that she wrote at Baxter. It was about two brothers that robbed a train in the old west and found themselves trapped on a never-ending ride and fighting over the only woman on the train.

The man, who must be a vampire, kicked his leg off the rail of the bench and sauntered over to Devin. His dark hair curled at his shoulders. His skin was as white as milk and his eyes as black as nothingness. He knelt down and got within inches of her face.

"So, you seem to know a lot about passion," he said.

He ran his thick-skinned dry finger down the front of her dress. He smiled wickedly. He smelled of sex and death. That same musty smell that Marisol carried like a badge of deathly honor. He leaned in closer and smelled the air around Devin.

She cringed back from the smell of him. She wanted to raise her hands and attack him. Maybe she could stun him just enough to make a quick escape.

"You smell like apricots my dear."

He leaned in closer. His fangs dropped pearly white from his lips. They were shorter than Julian's, but fierce none the less.

Devin shuddered her breath. He couldn't be thinking of feeding on her, could he? She held her breath and closed her eyes. She tightened her legs together and realized that the dagger was still safely strapped to her outer thigh. If she could just get to it, maybe she could stop him. She wished fear was not freezing her in that spot on the hard chair.

"Enough Danec!" a voice cracked from somewhere in the dark of the room.

He stood up and walked back over to the bench. He flopped down irritated and his face returned to human.

Devin knew that sound anywhere.

The *click click* of Marisol's heels echoed against the floor as she made her way to the center of the room.

"So, we are finally awake," she said to Devin.

She knelt down and lifted a dirty wet rag to Devin's temple. She shot back from the sting of the pain.

Marisol's face dropped into a pout. Fake sympathy. She did a terrible job of mimicking it.

Devin shook off the daze she was in and looked at Marisol. She held herself composed and ignored the numerous pains throughout her body.

"What the hell Marisol?" she yelled firmly.

"Ssshh, my dear. No yelling," she taunted back holding a finger up in the air. "Don't over exert yourself."

Julian, where are you?

"This is a bad situation for you," Marisol said. "You have been meddling in affairs that do not concern you. Julian, he does not always know what is best for him. He stalks his ex-wife, like a crazy person."

She gestures in the air and paced back and forth. She spins around on the heels of her shoes and drops back down to Devin's eye level. Her movements were so lyrical. Almost beautiful.

"Marguerite is not his anymore. She hasn't been for ages."

There was a strict tone in her voice that made Devin's heart skip a beat or two. She was sure that Marisol could hear each and every beat. She wondered if their hearts beat like the living.

"Marguerite belongs to us," Marisol said, altering her tone to jovial and standing back up. "Julian needs to learn where his priorities should lie," she brushes lint off her dress and rolls her eyes from the hem to her waist. Seeming acceptance of her appearance made. She looked back at Devin.

She is the priority, Devin thought. Marisol does want Julian. What is their story? Her journalist nature was banging on the inside of her skull.

Julian where are you?

Julian groaned and rolled onto his side. He felt the large lump swelling on the side of his head and coughed a few drops of blood onto the sidewalk. He grunted as he sat up.

He looked around for Devin, realizing she was gone, he jumped up. Shaking off the pain of small human injuries, he panned the street looking for any sign of her. He spots a small pool of blood by his feet. He can smell her. He can also smell Marisol.

"Damn it!" he screams, turns and takes off down the dark street back towards the Ptolemy Club.

His boots hard to the pavement in desperate rage. His coat billows out behind him in that breeze that follows him wherever he went.

"You were Julian's lover?" Devin asks Marisol.

"Lover? I was his *everything,*" she snaps her head back. "He, sometimes forgets how long ago he was married. How things have changed. How I was the one who gave him real life. He was miserable before he met me."

"So, he dumped you and now you're what…bitter?"

"Shut up! You know nothing about me."

"Then tell me. If you and Julian were such a great pair then tell me what happened."

Devin shifted in the chair uncomfortably. She struggled to show a comfortable look, even though the pain rolled on. She needed a brave face for Marisol. God she longed to know what went on between them. The lust rippling off Marisol was ripe and palatable. A million stories must be buried in that journal of Julian's. She wondered if Marisol kept one too. If they all did.

"It was many years ago. I was living in a squat with a bunch of friends. We did as we pleased, when we pleased. It was very retro, very hip."

"Very trashy," said Devin.

"Stop! You're such a little bitch. Don't you know when to keep you damn mouth shut?"

Devin locked her lips tight and paused in silence. Please continue she pleaded with her eyes. Any information may get her out of this crappy situation. Plus, she did not want to tempt fate and have Marisol decide it was time for a feeding.

"He came to me. He always will come to me. We spent night after night embracing the punk rock sub-culture outside the donut shop in the heart of alternative central. We were the couple to be. He wanted me completely. Everyone wanted me."

"But you wanted him."

Marisol's face was a glow like Devin had not seen before. She looked almost human.

"I did."

"And you went after him."

"We were each other's everything. I was a bit naive, but after all, I was still just a silly human then. Ha! A silly human like you. But he could not stay away. Once he made me…"

"You mean infected you."

"*Made* me a vampire. Then there was no stopping us. The carnage was legendary. We fed our way through the minions of the nameless and faceless. You have no idea how intoxicating the taste of blood mixed with Patchouli oil is. The lost ones. The ones no one would ever miss. Kind-of like you little one."

"So what happened to the great American love story? Did a hotter vampire come around? Did he bore of you like I assume everyone does eventually?" Devin chuckled.

Marisol's hand came down hard, slapping her back into reality. The pain stung, but she held a stoic face. Cannot show fear or pain.

"I left him. That is how I know he still pines for me you see. I left him broken. That will soon be clear once I rid myself of small irritancies. This is where you ask me what and I laugh and point to you darling!"

"But he doesn't want you. He wants Marguerite. You are just a shallow replacement. A ghost. A fake."

"He thinks his wonderful wife betrayed him. He will soon be made to see things clearly. See what Marguerite really is doing."

"You mean the scientists that Margaurite has been recruiting? The ones she wants to use to recreate the virus?"

Give it all away Devin. Geezzzz.

Marisol let out a loud powerful laugh. It echoed off the walls and the man on the bench cocked a short smile. Her demeanor changed with this new information.

"She is not recruiting anyone. She works for me. She *belongs* to me. This is hysterical. Julian has been hunting her for all the wrong reasons. He thinks she abandoned him for the others. He thinks that if he kills her, he will stop us. He's wrong. The others they took her against her will. They needed her. She has been, a pet, for a long time."

"Your pet?"

"Now, yes. But not always. It is too bad you won't be around long enough to learn all about our history. It *is* quite fascinating you know."

Marisol twists a strand of her long hair between her fingers playfully, like a child. She pouts lips and eyes at Devin.

"You mean *their* history."

Marisol shoots her a really pissed off look.

"*My* history! You think you know, understand, you know nothing."

"I know plenty. Julian told me everything about it and you. How you stalked him. How hurt you were when he dumped you. That you're lying right now about what happened."

God Devin hoped she was guessing right in making this stand.

"He stalked me. He wanted me. He is foolish enough to believe that Marguerite is in charge. What makes you think he wouldn't believe me?"

"He knows about Marguerite. He wouldn't be wrong."

"The big bad wolf wants her dead because he thinks she is the threat. In point of fact, she has been a pain in the ass for years and has always pined for her dark prince."

Devin could not believe it. All this time, Julian had thought that Marguerite was the enemy. That she had gone along with the crazy experiments. That she gave him up. He was wrong. She had to let him know. She had to break free and tell him, before it was too late.

"We could have killed her long ago, but instead the others saved her. Cared for her. Thought she would be of use."

A rattling sound came from behind Devin's line of sight. Slowly a figure began to come into focus.

"Ah, my dear," Marisol gleefully said, "You have come to join the party."

From the left of her peripheral vision, a small frail woman crept out of the darkness. Her face showed old fear and her eyes were wide open.

"Devin my dear, I would like to introduce you to your great grandmother, Marguerite."

Marisol outstretched her hand towards the frail woman, presenting her.

The women looked shocked. Her mouth puckered open slightly, as if she wanted to scream.

"Yes, I said she is family. Julian finally found the last of your children. He thinks this means he can re-enter our world and have a say. Ha! He was never that bright."

"Shut up," Marguerite spouted back. Her face quickly shifting to serious, just a Julian's could.

Marisol continued to chuckle, as if she was so above Marguerite that the possibility of an insult was so comedically poignant.

Marguerite knelt down next to Devin's chair and took her hand. Her skin was so cold, it shocked the warm blood in Devin's veins. She jolted her hand back. Then she saw the softness in her face. She looked like the old faded black and white pictures of her grandmother. She knew without question that she was in fact her blood. She mouthed the words *help me*.

Her hair spun in soft reddish brown curls all around her face. Her lips pouted slightly, as if all the blood left in her body was trying to force its way out in heavy words. Her eyes, how they ached.

There was so much that Devin wanted to ask her. What was Julian like when he was human? Why did they send Claudette to live with friends? What was the rest of her family like and where are they? So many questions she needed answers to. So much pleading she needed to do.

"Run along peasant. That is enough gawking for the day."

Marisol grabbed Marguerite by the back of the shirt and pulled her to a standing position. She spun her around a grabbed the back of her head and laid a big kiss on her lips. At first, she tried to struggle free from Marisol, but soon gave in to what was undoubtedly a common occurrence. Her hand slowly running down the length of Marguerite's top. Marisol then shoved her back off her feet and against the wall.

"Leave us!"

Laughter lilted out of her lips. Her assuredness in control of not only the situation, but everyone within it.

Marguerite paused as if she wanted to dive back towards Devin and hold her like a child. How Devin wanted her to. Marguerite wiped Marisol's thick red lipstick off her lips with the back of her hand.

"Out!"

She watched the frail figure scurry off the floor and out the door. Her last look was at the wooden chair.

"So, does it feel good to meet the rest of your family?"

Devin spit towards her fragile antique shoes.

"Julian never should have contacted you. I knew as soon as my father hired you, he would return to work. Occult expert my ass. Ha!"

"Your father?"

"Did I forget to tell you that part? Didn't you find it strange that someone as inexperienced as you would secure such a great job as a ghostwriter?"

That fact had always taunted Devin. She knew the day she was offered the job that she was less that qualified. After all, she was recently out of college and worked as a low-paid journalist for a neighborhood newspaper. She had not yet earned the skills and right to land such a huge opportunity. She hoped that maybe Baxter saw something wonderful in her and that is why he hired her. It was just a coincidence that they needed a ghostwriter when they met.

"Julian found you and killed your predecessor. My father hired you on *his* recommendation and light persuasion. Had I known about it, I would have stopped him."

"Who?"

"I am how they met, you know. After I was turned I introduced them. At first, my plan was to kill him. Leave his bloated disgusting body on top of his desk for the cleaning lady to find. To drain him from somewhere awful and painful. He had always been a terrible man. A con artist and sleaze ball wrapped in a tight suit full of lies. That picture above his desk says it all. But I soon realized that he could prove to be useful, so I allowed him to live."

A terrible truth began to consume Devin. There was just no way this could be true. No way this could be what she was hearing.

"Baxter?" Devin said with a trembling in her voice.

"Jake silly," she answered changing the tone in her voice to very jovial. "My name is Marisol Baxter. You work for my father."

Chapter Eleven

Julian's boots slammed hard against the cold dark street. His breath was coming out in angry huffs. The rage about him was almost visible as a violent streak down the pavement.

He powered up the few steps and busted through the door of the Ptolemy Club with one slick punch. He knocked the spiky haired boy down flat and let the heavy door slam behind him.

He shoved his way angrily through the room to the back secret curtain. He flipped it aside to see Leanna casually sitting at the large table with a young man kneeing on the floor beside her. His head was rested on her lap. She pet his hair like he was a cat. Even the blood traders of some of the powerful vampires had human slaves of their own.

"Stop right there dear," Leanna said emphatically, holding one hand up towards Julian and the other on the collar of the young man. She mocked a gesture to slit his throat.

"What do I care? He's just a human," Julian yells and pushed the man off her lap.

He scattered out of the room afraid and on all fours. Just like the pet he has allowed himself to become.

Leanna, now nervous herself, stands up and attempts to brush confidence back into herself with a quick brush down of her clothes. She stumbled to try and get a few words out. Pound for pound, he outmatched her severely.

Julian pressed his chest up against hers and held her to the wall. His heavy breath pushed the air out of her lungs and made her gasp softly.

"Where is she?" he spits into her face.

"I…don't know," she said in frightened reaction. "All I know is what Togo told me."

Togo, Julian thought, was Marisol's blood trader. Julian reached up and squeezed Leanna's throat tightly.

"And?"

"And Togo said that Marisol…wanted her. That she was a danger to their…work. Look, I don't know you, but I know them. You are an outsider Julian. You don't…belong here. You are an outcast."

He knew he was, but he couldn't let her know he believed it. He had been outcast so long he almost forgot that he was one sometimes.

"I am an original! Show some God damn respect!"

His hand slapped her cheek in a quick motion. A red mark began to appear immediately, as if all the blood rushed to that spot.

"Yes Julian, but you are an…outsider."

She grunted softly in pain. A drop of blood appearing over her bottom lip. Apparently, he had hit harder than he thought.

Speed things up, he thought.

He shook his head from side to side. He nighttime face exposed. He dropped his fangs into her shoulder blade once hard. Blood ripped from her veins and flowed down his throat like butter. His eyes rolled back into their sockets and warmth rose from his feet. He let go of her throat and let her slide down the wall unconscious. He turned and walked straight out of the club pushing aside anyone that got in his way.

He headed towards downtown, now hunting for Marisol. The sting of the head wound pulsed, but not nearly as fast as his adrenaline raced. The blood helped too. It gave him the energy he needed. God damn Marisol. He will end her this time.

"Baxter? What do you mean Baxter?" Devin asked.

"That is what I said. Are you too simple to listen? Too stupid?"

"Jake Baxter's daughter?"

"Yes."

So she must have taken Julian back to meet her father after she was infected. She must have taken him there to murder him. But, that means Baxter must know that Julian is a vampire. Why would he allow him to help her?

"And Baxter, I mean your father knows all about you and this...this world?"

"At first, I brought him there to kill my father, but soon realized, after his pathetic begging that he could be of use. Do you think he wears those cheap suits for no reason?"

"He gives you money?"

Marisol simply smiled.

"He gives me everything I demand. He has served his purpose to me for many years now."

"Julian is a good man. He is my family. I don't care about your past with him." Devin said with a hint of faked confidence.

She hoped that no one could see the terror that pulsed through her veins and the very real curiosity that gnawed at her.

What else didn't she know about Julian?

"A good man is the last thing he is and don't fret darling. I can see how eager you are to know about me. It is written all over your pathetic human face. I read you like a book darling."

"You are just jealous that he is not giving his attentions to you."

Marisol hissed. Devin knew that she had struck a nerve.

"You wish he was poking around at you and not just in your business."

"Enough," Marisol screamed. Her cold hand came down hard on Devin's cheek. It stung red. One more time and she might have to show the pain.

"Don't think I won't kill you right now where you sit you stupid silly girl."

"Julian would have your head on a stick."

That's it. Show her that you are not afraid. He will come for you. Just hold out. She breathed out a hefty sigh. He will come.

"I would just prefer to have the...pfft, dark prince... watch you die slowly. The last of his family. His last chance to re-join us on his terms. Once he realizes his mistakes, then he can come work for me or die."

Yeh, work for you, Devin thought. She was not interested in another night shift employee. She wanted him. It dripped off her like angry passionate sweat.

She seemed so aggravated. She turned and stomped out of the room without speaking. She snapped her fingers and the man on the bench got up and tied Devin's wrists tightly to the chair arms with blue silk fabric. He then followed her out the door. It banged hard against the frame.

She was alone in the room. Her heart beat furiously in her chest as she struggled to slide her wrists out of the ties. There was no use. They were tied with the strength of a vampire and although she fancied herself a part-time athlete, she was no match for that strength. She let out an exhausted sigh. Bad situation Devin. What was Marisol planning to do to her now that she is that mad?

Julian would come for her. She knew it. He had to. He was so desperate to find Margaurite and he could not do it without her? Could he? But what if he did come and found Marguarite and just killed her? Would he come and save her?

My God, this would make a terrific book. Damn it! Stop it Devin. Think this is serious. Stop thinking about the damn book.

Baxter is not who she thought he was. Her job was a set-up. Somehow Julian knew that she was family and managed to get her hired. This had all been planned out for years. What else didn't she know about?

Now, Julian was probably on his way here to kill Marguerite, while never knowing that she was not who he thinks she is. She is not the evil monster scientist trying to take over the world. She was a prisoner.

"Just like me," Devin whispered. "Just like me."

Julian pounded down the street. His lips were chilled and red like wine. Half from the lack of blood pulsing through his veins and half the adrenaline that did.

What was with Marisol anyway? What interest did she have in Devin? She couldn't know. There was no way. He could understand how angry she must be with him. After all, he was the one who made her. He made her into what she is. Years ago, stalking her quietly, befriending her, making love to her, until one night, taking her in Pebble Park. Draining her like a glass of fine wine. Covering her body with leaves as the night dripped over and the following sun arose. She was different and evil because of him. That can make a person angry. But why go through Devin to hurt him? And why interrupt his search for Marguerite? There had to be something there that he did not see. Something more to all of this.

As he neared his destination, his speed increased. He flew down the street in a blaze.

Reaching it finally, he powered up the stairs of the 1600 building. With one heavy pull, he ripped the door right off the handle. It banged against the sidewalk making small cracks in the concrete. He had plans for Marisol that did not include being gentle.

Why is she leaving me here alone so long? Wondered Devin. The strength of her standoff earlier had waned and now a bit of fear took over. Was she planning on turning her? Killing her? Where was Julian? Would the dagger safely hidden be enough to save her from unlife?

Silence.

Then there was the sound. A blaring alarm, like the building was in flames. *Beep beep beep beep.* She heard voices arguing in the halls and then the clack clack of Marisol's shoes entering the room.

"Get up!"

Devin grunted as she was yanked out of the chair. The restraints ripped right off the chair arms. Quickly they were refastened to her wrists. With a twist they were pulled tighter.

"We are leaving."

"Where are you taking me?" Devin struggled and pulled back.

"Somewhere your pretty knight in shining armor cannot find you precious. Somewhere to regroup. It's nothing dear."

A few steps down the hall and Devin was pushed into an antique elevator. Marisol slid the grated door closed and pushed the down button. A jolted start began to lower them.

"Anything you get is all your own fault," Devin said.

"Shut up. I don't need your mouth right now."

Marisol was fronting strength, but Devin could tell that something was terribly wrong. Marisol was noticeably nervous and maybe even a bit frightened.

The elevator stopped and a stern looking man opened the door. He gestured down the dark hallway. Devin's arm was grabbed and she blindly followed. It is obvious that strength will not get her out of this situation. Her smarts must. They started briskly walking towards an exterior door.

"He took out Jaysen and Brian. There was nothing that we could do ma'am. We all tried. He is just too fast and too strong. We need more guards."

"Are you all incompetent? How did he make it inside?"

"We are still trying to figure that out ma'am. We had all your precautions in place. Even the new alarm codes were active."

The stern man was built like a brick shithouse. His skin was deep chocolate and glowed. Maybe he was human. His shaved head gave him a scary look. Must be for effect.

"Is my car ready?"

"Yes ma'am."

His voice was so incredibly deep.

Just then a dark SUV screeched towards them. It stopped just short of hitting them and the doors flung open.

"Get in." Marisol demanded and pushed Devin towards the open door.

She climbed in and sat uncomfortably between Marisol and the large man. The constant chatter between 2-way radios told Devin that someone had broken into the building. Clearly, they were after them. Could it be Julian? Please let it be Julian.

"Don't assume it will be so easy for your stupid prince to find us," Marisol said. "Driver, head west."

"Yes ma'am."

"I have plans for you. Delicate violent wonderful plans."

She ran her cold fingers down Devin's throat.

"Do you want to know my plans?"

"Sure. Spill it."

Her face turned sharp and one of her nails grazed sharply along Devin's collarbone.

She winced from the pain. The hot stream of blood ran down between her breasts. She breathed in heavy. Cannot show pain. Cannot show fear.

Marisol ran her finger through the blood and raised it to her lips. She drank in Devin's scent.

"I get rid of you and he never re-enters our world."

"If you want him so badly…why…try to keep him out?" Devin grunts from behind the pain of the stinging cut.

"It is simple self-preservation dear. He has the ability to control Marguerite in ways no one else can. And she is the key to our developing the original strain. If I get that, I can make more *friends* you see."

"What do you want a little clan of followers?"

"An army. I want an army."

"Can't you just get Marguerite to do it for you?"

Marisol's face coughed in anger. Clearly Marguerite was not as keen on the idea of the creation of a vampire army.

"You cannot turn someone if you don't want to."

All the time that Marguerite had been a prisoner, she must have held out and not turned anyone. That is what Marisol is after. Someone who can make more vampires for her.

"If you re-create the original strain, then those infected can make more vampires?"

"Yes."

"What makes you think they will follow you?"

"Because *I* will be the one infected."

A clearer picture started forming in Devin's head. Marisol was not just looking to create the virus, but create one that infected those who already are vampires. So, she can create an army of their choosing. She would be just like those originally cursed. She would have the ability to create more vampires before the virus mutates. That is too much power for her to have, Devin twitched. She had to find a way to break free, to let Julian know what she planned. But how?

Julian powered down the hallway towards the room Devin had been held in. He ripped open the door and seeing that the room was empty, now knew they had already made their stealthy escape. Frustrated and angry, he heads back down the hall. Two men stand there blocking his way.

"Julian, this is not your night," one of the men said. He was short and round and clearly not human. He wore his fangs like a badge of honor. Julian imagined he never reverts to his human face.

"No, my friend, this is not your night."

Julian rushed at both men fiercely. Within seconds, the fat round one was dead on the floor. The other ran away as fast as he could. No use in chasing after him.

Julian left the building as quickly and loudly as he entered. The bloody bodies of human and vampire alike scattered the hallways. From the street you can hear the screams.

Thump.

"Driver, what the hell was that?" Marisol yelled.

"Not sure ma'am. I think we may have blown a tire. I'll take a look and let you know."

The SUV slowed to a stop and parked under a busted out streetlight. The neighborhood seemed mostly deserted, except for the few late night bar stragglers stumbling down the pavement. Their intoxicated state made them blind to the dangers just feet away. The driver got out of the front seat and closed the door. There was an eerie silence that hung for a few minutes.

"What is taking so long?" Marisol finally yelled and opened the side door.

"Driver!"

No response.

"Driver?"

Silence.

"Find that idiot driver," Marisol gestured at the large man pressed up against Devin's left side.

He grunted as he opened the car door and stepped outside. Now they were alone. The seconds ticked, until another grunting sound was heard. Marisol clearly heard it too. She looked back towards the hatch with a twinge of nervousness on her face. Before she could fully turn back around an arm swung open the door and ripped her clean out of her seat.

"Ahhh. Let go of me."

She was gone out of Devin's line of sight.

Sound of angry fists hitting hard bodies thumped outside. Devin knew this was her one chance. She tried to undo the restraints that had clumsily been tied. This was the one chance to break free. She managed to loosen one hand enough to help her sit up and climb into the front seat. She reached down towards the ignition and found the keys missing.

"Damn it!"

She carefully and quietly opened the door. Her feet made a soft crunching sound against the gravel. As she turned towards the back of the SUV, she saw him. The driver. It looked as if someone had tried to rip his face off. Devin slowly moved towards him.

Keys keys. Where would they be?

She winced as she lifted his heavy bloody dead arm.

He shuddered under her fingertips.

She dropped his arm and her heart stopped. She saw his fangs drop from his mangled face. He hissed softly, trying to regain his strength. He was a vampire.

Devin slowly reached under her dress and removed the dagger Julian had given her. She remembered him saying that if you cut the head off anything, it will die. The driver gurgled for breath, as Devin sat above him. She held the dagger in the air with both hand and brought it down hard against the driver's throat. His head snapped off like a soda pop cap. Devin was surprised at the force the dagger held or was it her own strength.

Now to find the keys.

"Need a hand?"

That voice. It was familiar.

Devin slowly raised her eyes up and saw Marguerite standing in front of her. She was covered in blood. She stood tall this time. Not like back at Marisol's place where she seemed to cower. She reached out towards Devin and ripped the remaining restraints off in one slick movement.

"Yes. Please," Devin responded, dropping the dead driver's arm.

Marguerite grabbed the man by the front of the jacket and practically lifted him up to a standing position. She reached into his vest pocket and retrieved the car keys. She tossed them to Devin.

"Thank you."

"Don't thank me. Take me to him."

By him, Devin knew she meant Julian.

"He thinks you betrayed him."

"I know."

"He might try to kill you."

"I know. Let's go."

Devin stood up and got behind the wheel of the SUV. Margaurite slid into the passenger seat and they moved down the street, back towards Devin's apartment. The one place she knew, he would come for her.

Kaytee Thrun

Chapter Twelve

Devin and Marguerite sat silently in her apartment as night crawled slowly along like a snail. The *tick tick* sound of the clock echoed so loudly that Devin was sure it would drive her insane.

Marguerite stared at the Macan painting for hours, seemingly mesmerized by the swirling of leaves and roses.

"Macan?" she asked.

"Yes."

"Did you know that when you bought it?"

"No. It just called to me."

"Then you have the extra gift. The sense we always assumed you would have."

"What sense?"

"The unspoken sense that allows you to feel our kind. It is something most of the commerçants de sang have in some fashion, but some more than others. We cannot explain why, but they just feel us. You have it, don't you?"

Devin thought about how every time a vampire was near, she felt this cool breeze and a subtle uncomfortable feeling. She always knew it meant something, but assumed everyone could feel it, but maybe just weren't aware of it. She also felt something crazy when she first saw the Macan painting. *Oil and blood*, Julian had once said about it. Maybe there really was blood mixed in there and that is what she felt drawn to.

"I guess I can feel it."

"You must use that feeling then. You must stop them."

"Why me?"

"Because it has to come from within. From inside the ranks, but not from one of us ourselves."

By *us* she must mean the originally cursed ones.

"From inside will come the end. We started it, I started it, and now you can end it. That you can do for us. Hunt the rest of them."

"How can I be a hunter?"

"Because you are. It is in your blood. My child. My legacy of darkness. My only gift to you in exchange for all the terrible things that came afterwards."

Marguerite reached out and held Devin's hand. It was like mother to child and Devin felt a safety she had not felt in so long, since moving to the city. She did not want them to die. She wanted to know her family. Her true family. She felt closer to Julian and Marguerite than she did her own parents. There was always a distance between them that she could never close. A vast ocean separating them, as if in some small way, they knew she was different.

"You know what you have to do Devin. Now that you know, you have to stop them. Julian and I cannot. We have never been able to, but you can."

"Did you ever even try?"

"Once. Once Julian and I stood alone against them. A terrible tragedy followed. My commerçant de sang, my sister, was killed right in front of me. And Julian's father, well that is a whole different story. They tortured him for days and made

Julian watch it all. He was never the same after that. It broke a big part of his soul. Our anger at their actions, their callous making of infected ones and their hunger to meddle with the virus destroyed our lives."

"But you eventually followed them."

"I did. I was lost and alone. Everyone around me was dying and I thought, maybe if I understood then things would be better. I was very wrong Devin. Julian though, never wavered in his hatred for them."

"That is why I need you both. You understand everything. I only know the little bit Julian has told me and what I have learned myself in this short time."

"We can't. We had our stand and lost. This family has already had enough sacrifices. It is time we passed the torch onto someone who can really do something."

"How?"

"As a blood trader you can get close to each of them. Take down their blood traders. Destroy the hierarchy."

"But I need your help. I can't do this alone."

"You can and you must. It is no longer my fight and it has never been Julian's."

"How is *my* fight?"

"Legacy my dear and I am so sorry for that. It is your family legacy to stop what we began so many years ago."

Take down the hierarchy. What did Marguerite think Devin was? She can't be a hunter. She didn't know how. With Julian at her side she could pretend, but for real. She wasn't so sure.

There were still a million things that she did not know. Things that Julian had not yet told her. A few stories and some kickboxing did not a hunter make. That seemed like too much, but maybe she owed it to Marguerite. Her blood. Her mind was so puddled with confusion.

Who are you now Devin?

She sat in silence, listening to that blood pulse in her veins. Her blood. Their blood. The blood of her true family.

They both sat. So long it seemed like time had stopped. The loud tick of the clock vanished and white noise engulfed the loft. Deafening silence all around.

Devin absorbed what Marguerite had said. How could she be a hunter? After all, she was not as strong as the vampires and she knew just a little about their world. The secrets were locked in Julian's journal. Maybe Marguerite knew that she was close to death. Maybe she knew what Julian would do. Maybe she knew about the journal.

"There is so much I need to know. This is all new. You have to understand, I don't want to lose you yet. I just found you and Julian. Please, just give me a little bit more time to know you both."

"You'll never lose us. We will always be part of you. We always have been. Your sense of us, your perception, your inquisitive nature, all those things came from us."

"How? Grandma Claudette was already born when you became vampires. Nothing could have been passed down."

Devin was looking for any excuse to remove herself from the fight she feared would soon come to her.

"When your grandmother was young, just after we realized what cursed life we would then lead, I made a terrible mistake. A mistake that made me realize that I must give away my baby in order to save her."

"What did you do?"

"I fed on her."

"You fed on your own baby?!"

"It is one of the things I regret most in my life and in my death."

Marguerite's head fell and she stared at the floor. A single tear slipped from the corner of her eye and splashed against the wood below. Devin swore she could hear it like a giant wave crashing against the shore.

"But obviously everything was ok. I mean, Grandma Claudette was fine. Everything was fine."

"She was fine, but slightly changed. Something in my horrific bite gave her a sense of who we are. A little bit of insight and strength. Stronger than the senses a normal blood trader has. That my dear, has been passed down to you. A dark legacy of death. It makes you stronger than the other blood traders. It is a gift."

Devin had always felt that something was different about her. She just assumed that her inquisitive nature and independence made her stand out in small town America. That is what made her want to leave. It made her enter the city like a bull into a stadium. To conquer. To achieve. But instead of living up to her legacy, she had been sitting alone in her loft writing romance novels and spending weeks engulfed in loneliness.

Had this all been a dark fate? Some magick?

"It's fate Devin."

"And Julian knows this?"

"He does. That must be why he found you. He knew you could find me much faster than he could on his own. Your senses added to the demanded rules of the vampire hierarchy."

"The blood traders."

"Yes. It always comes down to the blood Devin."

"You mean that without me, he could not have gained access to you?"

"Never. No one would have been permitted to speak to him. It's the rules of the covens. Plus, I presume you had to prove yourself worthy in the blood trader community as well."

"I did."

Boy had she. Devin longed to know more about this world. She dared ask small questions, hoping for just one tiny piece of information that would explain it all to her. Something that would make all this make sense after all.

"Why can only the originals make more vampires? Why does the virus mutate?"

"No one knows exactly. That most cursed piece of DNA vanishes. Becomes dormant."

"Has there been any luck recreating the original strain? That is Julian's biggest fear of you."

"There has been talk, but nothing that we know for certain. I think it is all bull shit myself. If it had been found, then we would have seen a change. A big change. Massive numbers of new vampires would have been born from Marisol and her followers. I think it is coming. But, who knows when."

Devin could sense that Marguerite did not want to talk about it anymore. She must have been made to do terrible things at Marisol's hands. Maybe she contributed to finding the original strain and does not know it yet. Maybe many died because of her protest and unwillingness to make more vampires. Stories were locked in her head as well. Stories that Devin would never have access to if she died. She would only have what Julian experienced and that was not enough for her.

They sat silently together as the minutes ticked by. Both in fear of hearing more about each other's lives and deaths and in wait of Julian's return.

Devin wondered in secret would that ever happen. Where was he if he did not find her and save her? Did he care enough to come back? Is he dead?

Then, just like clockwork, the sound of the front door creaking open stopped the air of silence that hung in the room. Julian's footsteps sounded deafeningly loud as he made his way over to where they sat. He reached out and wrapped his arms around Marguerite from behind. She closed her eyes and prepared herself, in case he decided to end her life right there. A half crooked smile lifted from her lips.

Julian breathed out a heavy sigh and held her. His rough hands on her shoulders. She reached up and put her hands on his. They melted together. Like finding respite after a long journey, they just paused together frozen in time. It was beautiful. A curl from behind Marguerite's ear fell in slow motion into her face. Julian reached up and retrieved it, tucking it safely back behind her ear. She smiled and turned to look at him. His face seemed so innocent, not dark as it usually is, but hopeful and loving. Just like her romance novels. Hope springs. They kiss.

Devin, feeling the cue to exit, stood up and walked into her bedroom. She knew they needed time alone. She also knew that if he planned to kill her, she could not bear to watch. She longed to know them, but understood the damning legacy that Julian wished to end. Maybe it was for the best.

Maybe this *was* her fight now.

Hours ticked by and Devin opened her tired eyes. She had fallen asleep on her bed. She looked over to the nightstand and read the clock that said 4:42 a.m. Sunrise would soon come. She had slept almost a full night. She must have been exhausted.

Fighting vampires must tire you out. Better workout than the health club she rarely went to, but paid for each month.

She placed her hands on the bed and grunted as she pushed herself up into a sitting position. She swung her legs over the edge of the bed and with one last push, stood up. She shuffled into the living room, half expecting to find two bodies lying on the hardwood floor.

No one was there. The room was eerily quiet and vacant.

She looked around for signs of a possible struggle. There were none. Nothing was moved. Nothing touched, as if they had never been there. For a split second, Devin thought that maybe this had all been a dream. Maybe that first night Julian did drug her and she is only now waking up after a long sleep. A small piece of her hoped for that. Hoped that all this had been a dream.

Then, she noticed it. It was just lying there on the coffee table. Julian's journal. His life for the past 15 or so years in pencil on parchment right there for her, just like he promised. She picked it up slowly, feeling the soft old leather between her fingers. It was smooth and well worn. It was real. She flipped through the pages and stopped randomly on one.

It is severely cold here in Chicago. I thought I would enjoy it more than I am. The cold air can be seen as it leaves my lips. It makes me feel alive. The last few nights on the streets have nearly beaten me down.

I spent the evening following around Maks. He has become even more vicious than we imagined. He took the lives of three small children tonight. He doesn't even bother cleaning up after the mess he makes. He simply left their bodies in the deep snow to be found in the thaw. I instead hid them in a warehouse. Hopefully, someone will retrieve them soon.

If the barmaid suspects him again, he could be caught and exposed. I don't know how he always seems to be able to slip out unnoticed. He risks exposing all of us. That cannot happen. He must be stopped at all costs. We must keep our dark secret from the humans.

Still no new word otherwise. I asked around the club for any information on Margi. No one has seen her. I think they are all lying. Lyllhit is interfering with my search. Her nature will get the better of her. It's time she met her demons. This time tomorrow, she dies.

Devin closed the journal. There must be hundreds, if not thousands of stories in here. Words that just begged to be ripped off the page and made real again.

Julian was right. This is his legacy.

She could write a hundred books off the haunting life he has lived. Maybe that is the true legacy that Marguerite should have spoke to. Not a hunter's legacy.

She turned and looked at the clock on the wall. It was 4:58 a.m. Almost sunrise. She had to hurry. She grabbed her coat and flew out the front door. It banged closed hard. She didn't bother locking it.

He always found a way in anyway.

She knew where they would be. She remembered Julian talking about spending one last moment in Pebble Park. If she ran, she just might make it there before the sun rose.

Her shoes clacked against the cement and echoed in the abandoned street. It was still too early for the neighbors to be awake. A few birds sang to her, almost in a funeral dirge. The air was muggy and the leaves dripped from the trees wet with dew.

She let out a heavy breath as she sprinted inside the park gate. The air was humid and heavy. A feeling she had grown accustomed to, after nights inside the Ptolemy Club. The hill was just up ahead. That had to be where they were.

Her breath was now painfully lumped in her throat. As she made the ascension, she saw two figures standing together holding hands. It was Julian and Marguerite. They heard her coming and turned towards her.

"You...can't...please stop," Devin spurted out with short breaths and she slowed her sprint to a walk.

"Dev, this is what is right. We go out together, as one. Just as we should. Just as we became what we are," Julian said.

His face told her one story, but something was wrong about this picture to Devin. She couldn't put her finger on it, but something did not seem right.

"But I hardly...know you. Please, I want to know you both."

She reached out towards them, as if she could magically pull them back in from this terrible fate. That maybe her blood would make them stay just a little longer. Some family obligation that had been passed off to strangers so many years ago.

"You will know us," Julian said and gestured towards the journal still locked tightly in Devin's fingers. "You will know me more than I could ever explain. The good and the bad of me. The truths that I could never bare to tell you myself. Your real family. And then you can decide if you want to remember us or not. The choices will all be yours."

"I...already know that answer. I already know you and I know that I need to know more. From both of you, please."

Devin's breath was starting to return to normal. She took another step towards them almost in an unspoken last plea.

Marguerite opened her arms and embraced her. Devin melted into her bosom like an infant. A tear rolled down to her lips. Salty. She longed to stay in that moment forever. She had not felt this safe is years. Ever since she moved to the city alone. Her parents never made her feel this safe. Their life had been filled with uncertainties and money problems. Life was never safe.

"We always will be a part of you. Remember what I told you," Marguerite whispered and kissed the top of her head.

Julian reached out and hugged Devin quickly. He could barely handle the good-bye. As they broke the embrace, he took Marguerite's hand and turned back towards the overlook. They stood there waiting for the encroaching dawn to come and carry them away.

Devin wondered how long it would take for them to die. She wondered if it would be instant and blasting like on television or if it would take minutes or hours to fully kill them. Julian once told her that they could withstand a few minutes of direct sunlight, but that was all. She wished them no pain in death, as they had so much in unlife.

"It's time for you to go Dev," Julian said.

She knew it to be true, but didn't want it to be.

He gestured back towards the entrance of the park. He did not want her to witness the terrible fate that had come to pass.

She turned around, away from the hill. She knew he was right. She could not bear to see them when the sun rises. It would be too painful a sight. She could already feel the painful ache in her chest. Her heart was purely breaking.

The worn leather of Julian's journal melted into her fingertips. Soft. Like his words. Rough. Like the truth. But family still and these pages were all she had left. How can she go on now? The reality of Baxter Publishing and the truth of her deadly inheritance could never be erased. She could not go back. It was too late. And her parents, who are they really? If not her parents. Her grandparents. She wondered if any of them knew these terrible secrets.

She repeated a truth in her head that she always held to. We all do need three things in this life. Something to feed our heart, something to feed our soul, and something to feed our pocketbook. Devin clutched the journal tighter. This journal would now feed her pocketbook. Her wallet. Hundreds of books could flood out if it like water. Each one with the soul exposed on the page, not like the romance she scribbled. Her own personal writing always fed her soul. Her heart felt like it was breaking. She felt so empty.

She knew the slow death approaching behind her on the hill. Nothing fed her heart now. It was black and cold. Her deathly legacy more apparent than it had ever been before. How could she possibly live up to what Marguerite and Julian expected of her? How could she possibly be what they wanted her to be?

The world had forever changed for her, ghostwriter and now vampire hunter. A deathly legacy, she thought. A blood legacy.

She exhaled as her shadow drew out in front of her slowly. Her subconscious self stretching out from her feet in the darkness. The sun slowly crawls its way into existence behind her. Creeping up over the hill like a killer. It heats her back as it rises. She knows death is just a few feet away and this time, she cannot save anyone. She must simply stand and be strong.

"Good-bye," she whispers to no one in particular.

And as always, there is nothing but silence.

The End...for now

Remember to thank those
who inspire you…

KT

About the Author

My love affair with creating began when I was a child. I used to spend every afternoon in my parents' floral and antique shop. As the only daughter of an artsy floral designer father and a crafty teacher mother, I was always able to see the beauty and potential in even the strangest things. On one trip to an auction with my parents, we came home with a rickshaw, a wicker coffin, a king's sword and scepter, and a laboratory skeleton. Many days like that one fueled my imagination and eccentricity.

In high school, my art teachers were great inspirations for me. They allowed me to go off-curriculum in every class from photography to painting to metalsmithing and explore bringing to life the crazy images in my head. You see, I was one of those weird kids that hung out with the artists, skaters, theater kids, and outcasts. With that and a very liberal upbringing, I was able to learn about nature, art, gemstones, self-expression, tarot, writing, and something wicked that came this way…

In my years, I have dabbled in all types of art from interior design to poetry to watercolor. They all allow me to bring a feeling or an image to life through art that can be shared everyday with everyone around you. Now, I am a grown woman that does not regret the roads I have walked down or the amazing sights I have seen along the way. I have found my own extraordinary side and I hope I can help you find yours. I hope that you will find a piece of my work that will inspire you to be who you are.

Kaytee

www.kayteethrun.com

Notes From The Ghostwriter

October City Vampire Tales, Volume 1

Copyright © 2007 *Kaytee Thrun*

ISBN: 978-0-6151-3883-1

www.octobercitypress.com